A Day
in
San Francisco

A Day
in
San Francisco

a novel by
Dorothy Bryant

Ata Books
Berkeley, California

Ata Books
1928 Stuart Street
Berkeley, California 94703

Cover Design: Robert Bryant
Production Assistance: Kathy Vergeer and Anne Fox
Typesetting: Ann Flanagan Typography

Oh my son Absalom, my son, my son Absalom!
Would God I had died for thee,
O Absalom, my son, my son!

II Samuel 18:33

I have set before you
life and death, blessing and cursing:
Therefore choose life

Deuteronomy 30:19

*For John
who chose a happier path*

Eight white men in black nuns' habits plucked up their skirts between thumb and forefinger, swishing them from side to side above red satin petticoats. Kicking their thin, black-netted legs, they pranced and wobbled on their spike heels. Their faces poked through loose, lopsided wimples, pale and taut, though their red lips opened wide with seductive smiles. As they squinted into the hard, white glare of the fog, their mouths stiffened into the clenched smiles of footsore chorus girls.

Clara winced in sympathy. Remembering the days of obligatory high heels, she almost felt the electric pain shooting up her own legs. She thought of some of her students, who, taking for granted the hard-won right to wear pants on all occasions, now chose to wear high heels with their jeans. Her warning against this self-betrayal would seem only puritanical or an expression of kill-joy envy of younger women. She wished they were here to let the "sisters" laugh and tease them into getting their feet planted solidly back on the ground.

Suddenly the "sisters" broke into a galloping, tripping run, trying to cross Fifth Street before the light changed to let traffic cross the path of the parade. Too late. They were stopped by a policeman who turned his broad back on their jumping dance and on the lewd gestures they made toward him. Though cheered on by the crowds, they gradually quieted until only two of them were making slight knee twitches, like marionettes jerked by impatient children.

Their entrapment gave Clara half a minute to study the flutter of their heavy false eyelashes, the occasional flick of their black skirts to flash the blood-red ruffles under them. There were layers of meaning to contemplate in these young men disguised as taffeta-ruffled whores disguised as black-robed nuns: two quaint versions of women no longer extant, stereotypes even when they did exist.

The light changed, and they lurched forward, followed by thirty young women, neatly dressed, like Clara, in jeans with print shirts under bulky sweaters. Most wore their hair short, as she did. The sign identifying the group of women remained hidden by the thick crowd, which tended to drift into the street, people weaving around each other to get a better view. Clara caught a glimpse of a smaller sign GAY PATRIARCHY IS STILL PATRIARCHY. Then the gap closed again, hiding it. There was no response to the sign. The spectators, mainly clusters of short-haired, muscular men in T-shirts and jeans, turned to talk, to shoulder or embrace each other playfully, until something that interested them should pass. A few in the crowds were, like Clara, fiftyish and alone. She saw few man-woman couples, and no children, until another gap briefly opened in the crowd.

A woman and a ten-year-old girl marched alone, in matching blue shorts and shirts, a matching bluish cast to their bare legs in the cold fog. They walked hand in hand, each with a sign pinned across her chest. Clara could not read the child's sign, but the woman's said A GAY PARENT. Then the little girl turned, and Clara could read the sign which proclaimed her A HAPPY WELL-ADJUSTED CHILD. Clara smiled and sighed, her eyes drawn back to the mother with envy of her bravado, her assurance, her innocence. Well-adjusted. Where did this young woman dig up the term? It was almost as quaint as stereotypical nuns and whores. Clara imagined herself and Frank in the place of that mother and child. Would he wear a sign stating GAY MAN, while she wore one that proclaimed her A WELL-ADJUSTED PARENT? Clara smiled at her little joke, which would probably remain hers alone, unshared with Frank, who had told her years ago that straight people did not march in the Gay Freedom Day Parade. It was different from the demonstrations he and Clara had joined to support racial and political minorities. Even her presence as a spectator was unnecessary.

A small group of men and women carried signs reading GAYS AGAINST NUKES. Clara clapped her hands as they passed, but few other spectators seemed to notice them. The last time she and Frank marched together against war, twelve years ago, he suddenly ran off to join a contingent of gays, the first Clara had seen in any demonstration.

Now it seemed as if the tiny gay contingent had swallowed up the whole parade, then swelled to a huge procession that surpassed Saint Patrick's Day and Chinese New Year, and any political rally in Clara's twenty-year participation. From the foot of Market Street to Civic Center, crowds filled the sidewalks, windows, and roofs to cheer gays from Hawaii in grass skirts, gays from Canada under maple leaf banners, gays from Fresno on a star-spangled float. The little anti-war group was lost in the cheer that rose to greet the float of caged, chained, bare-chested men labeled PITBULL BATHS.

"...end of the world...son...my son...Jesus said if you...straight to hell...filth and damnation, my son... my son...."

Clara turned toward the wobbly, chanting voice. The woman stood behind her. She was about seventy, with pale, soft skin and yellow-gray hair. She wore a neat, bright green raincoat, buttoned and belted around her thick body. "...thirty pieces of silver a month to kill...afraid Dan White would be mayor and protect...while this world burns...if the people of Sodom don't...abominations...Jesus said...hell and...." Her words bunched up behind one another, a rapid, slurred monotone in a weak but steady voice broken by sudden gusts of wind that carried words away, leaving short gaps between phrases. "My son...son in sin...."

Clara looked around to see whom she was calling her son, but the woman seemed to be addressing at random any of the men who glanced toward her and then quickly turned away. A few started to laugh, then stopped with a weak smile and a shrug; she was mad. Yet her eyes looked only tired, even bored, as she stared at the backs of the spectators between her and the parade she could not see as she called it "desecration...my son...repent...." Even had the old woman been a sane heckler, no one would answer her taunts. The mood of the crowd was too cheerful, ruled by an unspoken determination to let nothing mar the mellow frivolity of both paraders and spectators.

Suddenly the sun broke through the overcast sky, as if to mock the woman, and a loud cheer drowned her out. The cheer was not for the sun, but for the hundred women marching under a gleaming yellow and white banner LESBIANS OFF ALCOHOL. They were singing to the old jazz tune:

> When the dykes go marching in
> When the dykes go marching in
> We're going to get there sober
> When the dykes go marching in.

Clara clapped and cheered too, wishing that some of this brave joy could be injected into the North Counties Alcohol Project. Her Bay Area friends were always astonished when she told them the extent of alcoholism up there, as if the beauties of stately redwoods and rugged sea cliffs made unemployment easy to bear. To them it was a joke that a major industry was illegal marijuana cultivation. But it was no joke to attract even desultory attention of law enforcement officials, or, when the crop was good, the more sinister attention of encroaching big crime interests. No wonder so many of her neighbors preferred the solace of a bottle to sober confrontation of these paradoxes. Certainly Clara held no answer, but if some of this spirit could be exported...she made a mental note to contact someone in this group. Perhaps that laughing black girl waving the far end of the banner would come up and speak at a meeting.

"...thirty pieces of silver...locked him up...to save us from the supervisor from Sodom...." Clara decided to listen more closely. This mad woman's message, whatever tangled mass of ugly prejudice it might be, was the only reference so far to the assassination of The City's liberal mayor and gay supervisor. But the ranting woman was drowned out again by laughter as a girl pedaled past on a unicycle, each hand resting on the shoulders of her two companions, a man and a woman. The sign around her neck read A BISEXUAL BUILT FOR TWO.

A gap opened in the thickly packed crowds. Clara could see to the other side of Market Street, where huddles of men stood smiling, eyes left, looking toward coming amusements she could not see. One man turned to another and said something that exploded a whole group. Some threw back their heads. Others bent double, holding their sides. Two threw their arms around each other and hung helpless with laughter. Hilarity died down, then shifted to another group where the process was triggered again by a word or a gesture. How strongly they reminded Clara of her high school days. They even looked like the boys she had known. It must be their hair, she thought, tightly shorn, almost to the scalp. The moustaches—they all wore small moustaches—were a modern touch. No one had worn moustaches back then, so soon after Hitler.

Now, as then, Clara stood outside their hilarious camaraderie, watching. She looked from face to face, not really expecting to see Frank among them, though he must be here somewhere, assuming he had gotten over the flu. His fever had dropped two days ago, and in his last phone call he had told her he was determined to be at the parade. Would she recognize him easily in the crowds? He could not have changed much in only a year. His abundantly black-curled head would tower over most of these men.

"...damnation-purgation-purfication illuminating the Lord's white angel avenging...."

The steady monotone was overcome by yells, hoots and whistles greeting the DYKES ON BIKES. One radiantly smiling girl rode with her brown arms in the air, her long tawny hair streaming behind her. Others sat more squarely on their motorcycles, stolid as John Wayne on a horse. Groups of two or three stopped, revving up their motors, then sprinted forward again. In dusty, grating gusts, the women roared past while rows of men shrieked, waving both arms with fists clenched.

12

The noise hit Clara like a shock wave, pushing her back a step. Men crowded into the space she left, and she was pushed further back, bumping against the green-coated lady who, ignoring Clara's apology, continued to spout, "Hell and damnation, corruption...but the vengeance of the Lord...."

Spinning off the relentlessly ranting woman, feeling pursued by her, Clara almost collided with a man carrying a stack of *Gay Streets*. A lucky accident: an article or interview by Frank was to be in this issue. She would be able to read it before she saw him. The man carrying the newspapers looked through Clara, his judgment of her—old and straight—making her invisible, no potential customer. She had to poke the dollar at him and tug before he released a paper with a surprised half smile. No wonder so many old faces seemed set in expressions of anger or apology. Clara wondered what would happen to her own face if encounters like this were not balanced by relations with her students, who respected the mind behind the wrinkles. Perhaps the ranting crazy-lady had found her own solution to a couple of the problems of old age, achieving not only visibility but an uneasy kind of deference.

Clara glanced at her watch, then turned in the direction of the BART station, opening the paper as she walked. The motorcycles had receded so that the old woman's voice rose clear with "...the white angel of destruction sent by the Lord to the sons of Sodom on the day when...."

The rest was drowned out as the Gay Freedom Day Marching Band strutted past, playing and singing, "If My Mom Could See Me Now..."

"DOCTOR DICK"

An interview with Richard Wayne Hartzler
by Frank Lontana

The office of Doctor Richard W. Hartzler is in the basement of his home on 42nd Avenue, that bastion of family life and homophobia which lies swathed in thick fog throughout the summer (while the sun shines on Castro Street). The walls of his office are dark-stained knotty pine, like the unused bar in the corner. Clearly this is an old "rumpus room" like the one my aunt put into her similar home when I was a child. Bookshelves have been added and half filled with a curious mixture of psychology text-books, inspirational self-help paperbacks, and biographies of television celebrities. The rest of the shelves and the top of the bar are stacked with a jumble of papers and magazines: Moral Politics, Family Times, Christian Mental Health, *and, of course,* Moral Morale, *the newsletter put out by the famous Reverend Nathaniel Gynt. On the small desk sits only a large photo of Hartzler's wife and two young daughters. Despite the green rug on the floor and the glowing electric heater, the room feels damp and chill, so I keep my coat on. Hartzler, in shirt sleeves, seems quite comfortable as he tells me to sit down in one of three Danish chairs. Then he leans back in the swivel chair at his desk and demands that I call him Dick.*

So be it. Dick is—to my gradually diminishing astonishment—thirtyish, and looks younger. He is slim and agile in tennis shoes (propped on the desk), jeans, and checkered shirt. With his long face, aquiline nose, and black hair, he looks disconcertingly like me, except for his buttoned-down collar and relentless smile. His lips curve upward perpetually, like a permanent face lift, as he waits for my first question.

Frankly, Dick, I wonder why you would consent to an interview by a hostile publication. Aren't you afraid your statements will be distorted, ridiculed?

I quit worrying about that after my trial. I learned there was nothing I could do about it, so if I want to reach people, I just have to be completely open and not worry about things I have no control over.

Let's start with the article that was in the Chronicle *last month. In it you are quoted as saying that families with gay children should disown them. Is that an accurate quote?*

Not completely. I said that being rejected by his family can have a good effect in stubborn cases because it throws the client completely upon the therapist, making counseling more effective.

This article also says you do aversion therapy, like electric shock or

No, that was inaccurate. I sometimes refer a client to someone who does aversion therapy, if the client requests it, but I don't do it myself.

What treatment do you offer?

I prefer the word counseling.

Is that for legal reasons?

Partly, yes. I try to use the best of all counseling systems, whatever is useful in each individual case. If necessary I work with the client alone, but whenever possible, I use family sessions, getting the homosexual together with his parents, siblings, spouse, other relatives or even friends. Then we explore causes behind the homosexual behavior. For instance, there might have been sex role confusion, if the mother was dominant in the home, or if she was working outside the home. Which also could involve lack of proper supervision, so the child was prey to some perverted adult who drew him into homosexuality. Or, in many cases, a very permissive home left the child with no strong moral anchor or clear set of standards.

You consider these to be the causes of homosexuality?

Some of them, yes.

What about genetic causes? The latest Kinsey Report concludes that some people might simply be born

I reject that theory completely. Of course, it's very popular among homosexual scholars, for obvious reasons.

What reasons?

They want to prove that homosexuality is incurable. Because then they can say it's normal, even superior to heterosexuality—an evolutionary step forward beyond the family—an answer to overpopulation. They insist that it is inherent, natural, desirable because it suits their purposes.

What do you mean?

You know what I mean. There are obvious advantages in homosexuality.

What would you say those advantages are?

Freedom from responsibility. A heterosexual marries, has children, has to worry about his wife, has to walk the floor with crying babies all night, has to support his family, educate them, guide them. There's the legal bond of marriage and parenthood that can be very tough if the marriage develops problems. There's the complex relations with in-laws.

Isn't the choice to remain single and childless open to heterosexuals too?

There's less pressure to marry if you declare yourself homosexual. Or to stay married. Before the gay lib movement, some homosexuals had children and carried more or less their share of the responsibilities of family life. Now, they're coming out of the closet and deserting their families. So we're talking about a very convenient inversion syndrome.

What about gay couples who lead monogamous, hardworking lives together, just like other people?

Oh, not like other people, infinitely easier. Heterosexual life is more complicated. A person has to relate to all different kinds of people, with mixtures of complex traits. It's much easier to relate to someone who is just like yourself.

Are you saying gay people are all alike?

More so than normal people.

Normal meaning straight. Straight meaning normal?

Haha, Frank, trying to trip me up? Of course, heterosexuals may have other mental disorders. Homosexuality is just one of many character disorders. It happens to be one which affords a number of advantages and temptations, perhaps more than other abnormalities. Like pleasure. Without responsibilities, the homosexual has more time to devote himself to the pursuit of empty pleasure.

You think pleasure is bad?

Disproportionate amounts of pleasure—instead of work, responsibility, taking up one's share of the burdens of running the world.

Frankly, you do make straight life sound grim. Do you think it is possible that some straight people—with burdens—could be a little bit envious of gays? And that could account for their hostility toward gays?

No mature, balanced person could envy gay life. But there is some temptation for the young, naive person who doesn't realize that the price for that freedom and pleasure is too great.

What is that price?

Self-respect, primarily.

You think gay people lack self-respect?

I know they do. The people who come to me are often on the brink of suicide.

That would be true for any therapist, wouldn't it? Only those who are troubled come, so there's a selection process.

Gay people who aren't troubled have only repressed their consciousness of their condition, so they're worse off than the troubled ones who come for help.

By your standards, I'm really sick.

But never beyond help, Frank.

Well, let's get back to the advantages of being gay, before my condition improves and I slit my wrists. Any more advantages?

It's a handy mask for hostility. Homosexuals are full of anger. You see this breaking out in their demonstrations, which provoke reaction and lead to violence.

You don't see demonstrations as reactions to real oppression, for instance, like the murderer of Harvey Milk getting a light sentence, like harassment by thugs or by police?

No, that's just an excuse to release pent-up anger.

Anger against whom?

Sometimes their families, sometimes the whole society. Homosexuals are always saying how much prejudice they suffer, but they are only projecting. Homosexuals are much more prejudiced than heterosexuals.

I don't follow that.

Well, homosexuals make up about five percent of the population, and they're prejudiced against the other ninety-five percent. So they're much more prejudiced than heterosexuals, who are only prejudiced against the five percent.

I still don't follow you.

I know. Your own prejudice is bound to make this hard for you, Frank. In any case, homosexuals start with releasing hostility by engaging in practices that outrage and weaken society. Then, when society disapproves, the homosexuals can come out with even more direct hostility in protest marches demanding the right to outrage society.

Do you believe that about all protest movements? What about the women's movement? There's been a lot of anger expressed by women rejecting their traditional role.

Yes, and the core of the women's movement is lesbian, isn't it? So I think that proves my point.

I confess, I've lost track of your point. Let's try another question. What do you think about men like Oscar Wilde, W.H. Auden, Gore Vidal, Leonardo da Vinci, E.M. Forster, Chris...

Oh, yes, the creative homosexual, the genius. I agree, the homosexual artist has a certain advantage.

You think so?

Oh, absolutely, there's that excess sexual energy diverted, in the case of these men, into works of art.

You're saying gays have a stronger sex drive?

No, but since they never experience the total release of heterosexual sex, never achieve true normal orgasm with its relaxation of the nervous system, they have a constant excess of unresolved sexual energy which frequently drives them to unusual accomplishments in their chosen field. You look dubious, but this is all very well documented. I haven't time to look up the references for you right now, but I'll be happy to do it later and give you a call and name some sources.

Do these sources cite their own experience, comparing same-sex lovemaking with opposite-sex lovemaking?

No.

What about your own experience? Have you had gay sex and compared it with making love to your wife?

Never. (Laughs) Have you ever had sex with a woman?

Never. But I know gay men who have, and they contradict what you say.

Well, Frank, of course, they would.

Let's go back to questions about treatment—excuse me, counseling, again. Is it true that you require your clients to be celibate?

Not celibate, just not homosexual. I require that they agree to stop homosexual practice while undergoing counseling.

Isn't that a rather stiff requirement?

Not as stiff as most people think. With all the emphasis on sex, we forget that many people have chosen celibate lives without any ill effect, in fact with great effects. Some athletes are celibate in training. Some artists remain celibate while working. Many religious... and look at Gandhi.

Are you suggesting celibacy is superior to any sex?

It may be. That's not proven yet, and not possible for most of us, not for life. But I require that my clients make the effort to meet me half way. If they're serious about it, they can do it.

What if a client of yours stayed celibate for a while, then came to a counseling session and told you he'd picked up a man the night before and had sex. What would you do, end therapy right there?

Now you're referring to my trial.

Yes and no. I'm curious about what you would do, right now, in such a situation.

Well, it would depend. If he slipped once, regretted it, then we could try to work it out. But in actual practice, anyone who accepts that condition of therapy, then breaks it, just doesn't come back again.

Given a client who has agreed to remain celibate or to try heterosexuality, what methods do you use?

Oh, everything from the most standard counseling techniques to hypnosis and prayer.

You pray with them?

My colleague, Reverend Gynt, uses that approach. His background gives him a certain expertise and authority. Most men of our generation, Frank, come out of a completely atheistic background. To try to bring back some spiritual support to the mind is an essential step in returning to mental health.

I thought many gays came from strict church backgrounds.

When that's the case, we do have something to build on.

This alliance with Reverend Gynt—you see it as a proper connection for a psychologist?

Of course. You know what psychology means—the study of the soul. A lot of people forget that, narrow it down.

I see you have copies of Reverend Gynt's magazine, Moral Morale. *You subscribe to his views?*

Not all of them. We have enough common ground to work together but reserve the right to differ sometimes.

Reverend Gynt has stated that homosexuals should be put in prison. Do you agree with that?

I believe in obeying the law, and the law in most states still defines homosexuality as a crime.

Reverend Gynt cites the Bible *as above all laws, as authority for calling gay people criminals, whatever the laws of the state may be. Doesn't he say something like "Sin is crime"?*

Now I don't go that far. As a psychologist I see sin as only partly choice, partly sickness. And if a person just starts to lean toward choosing cure, I'll go all the way

with him. Even the toughest case, with the will on his part and patience on mine, can be cured.

But if a person isn't willing to be "cured," then would you agree with Reverend Gynt that he should be put in prison?

Yes. A lot of sick people have to be locked up, to protect society. Murderers are often sick people, you know.

You lump homosexuals and murderers together?

It's a matter of degree, isn't it?

Degree of what?

Of violence done to the stability of society, violence done to its deepest values.

Maybe this would be a good point to have you tell us more about your background. You were born in South Dakota and grew up there?

That's right. A little town called North Russ. My father was minister of the local Baptist church.

I thought he was a teacher.

Part-time, yes. It was a tiny place, so he taught at the local school, and was minister, and farmed a little too. Until the new high school was built. Then he taught full time; just retired last year.

After high school, you didn't go to the University of South Dakota?

No, I attended Swam Institute for a year.

Is that a four year college?

No, two year. A sort of business school.

So after a year you left Swam Institute. You attended two other colleges, didn't you?

Three.

But you didn't stay long in any of them. According to my research, you withdrew with failing grades.

Oh, yes. Have you ever been so turned off by a curriculum and your professors that you just couldn't bow down to them?

Yes.

Then you understand. I was searching. You know, that's what the life of the mind is, a great search. And when your search leads you into dry, rigid, theoretical corners, then you have to turn away and continue the search elsewhere. Now I don't regret the time I spent in those institutions. I learned something. I always learn, from everything that happens. I'm learning a lot just talking to you, Frank.

You came to San Francisco about five years ago?

That's right.

And you set up here as a therapist.

Counselor.

Counselor. But you call yourself Doctor. You're not an M.D.?

No. I have a Ph.D. in psychology.

Your Ph.D. is from Hettlebush University in South Pine, Mississippi. Isn't that one of those diploma mills?

It offers study through correspondence. Independent study.

Is it accredited?

No.

You've never seen the campus?

No.

Your Ph.D. came in the mail.

Yes.

Do you belong to any professional organizations in your field?

No.

Did you ever?

Yes.

What happened?

You know what happened, Frank. The association refused to renew my membership after my trial.

How did that affect you?

Professionally not at all. Personally I was disappointed that they would discriminate against me. But men who go against the crowd have always been persecuted, haven't

they? Like many organizations and institutions, that one has come under the control of homosexuals.

Reverend Gynt says "homosexuals and Jews."

Yes, but I don't go all the way with him on the Jewish thing. Some of my best friends are Jewish.

Perhaps we should review the court action we've referred to, in case some of our readers don't know. Do you mind talking about it?

I welcome the opportunity to give my side of it to your readers. In 1976—four years ago—I was counseling a young man who told me he was homosexual. I advised him to stop, and he refused.

Had he come to you for counseling about his sexual preference?

No, it was about another matter. But I saw that the two problems were linked, that I couldn't help him with one if he wouldn't work on the other. He refused, so I terminated counseling.

Abruptly. In the middle of a session.

Yes.

What was his reaction?

He was upset.

Did he threaten suicide?

Yes. But, as you know, he didn't carry through that threat. He reported me to the State Board of Health, to the District Attorney—for practicing medicine without a license—and to the ethics committee of the Association of Counseling Psychologists. The D.A. refused to press charges, so he sued me for personal injury, with the backing of a gay rights group. I won, of course, but it took nearly a year and cost over eighty thousand dollars. I didn't have eighty thousand, I didn't even have one thousand. I'd only been here a year, and my wife had just had our second daughter.

How did you raise the money?

By lecturing, by talking about my trial, and about the principles I stood for in counseling homosexuals.

Had you given lectures on these principles before? Or written papers on them?

No, they began to develop out of this experience, out of the great response to my ideas, the need of the layman for guidance.

Here in the Bay Area?

There's not much of an audience for my point of view here. I'm just back from a tour of mid-western states.

So, out of the publicity surrounding the suit, you found an audience for lectures. And then you decided to limit your counseling to homosexuals exclusively.

That's right. I didn't seek it. It was thrust upon me. Requests just poured in.

And this was how you began your association with Reverend Gynt?

Yes. We met when I was lecturing to a group of parents in Nevada. Actually I had met him years ago at college. He taught a course on the *Bible.* He has since retired and come west. He was leading a campaign to stop the flood of homosexual pornography being mailed to boys. We had a few talks, then decided to work together, pooling our knowledge, fusing those two parts of the study of the soul that have been so long separated—science and theology.

But Reverend Gynt doesn't live here.

No, he remains based in Nevada, but flies in, or I go there several times a month. He handles arrangements for my speaking engagements in other states.

Would you say your name is a good drawing card because of the publicity surrounding the suit against you?

Yes, that's true.

Isn't your most frequent lecture called "Immunizing Your Child Against Homosexuality"?

That's a popular one, yes.

What does it consist of?

Basic principles of providing healthy family life, proper role models, a strong religious life. I'd be happy to give you a copy to take with you.

And Reverend Gynt lectures with you?

Sometimes.

What else does he do?

Well, that depends.

Isn't it true that Reverend Gynt works mainly on a form of therapy called Sexual Exorcism?

We don't use that term anymore. Reverend Gynt chose it because of his theological bent, but I feel it was a bit strong. Unscientific.

So what do you call it now?

Oh, I dislike labels.

Hasn't it also been called deprogramming?

That term has popped up, but it's not really my first choice.

Is it true that you frequently cross the state line to join Reverend Gynt in deprogramming sessions, and that this deprogramming involves forcing a man to look at Playboy *nudes while Reverend Gynt reads biblical threats against sodomy?*

Now that's a terrible exaggeration. You make us sound very crude, but it's not like that, I assure you. It's very eclectic, depending on the needs of the individual client. I don't really think I can give a complete explanation in a short interview. Mainly it's just a series of more intense counseling sessions.

You kidnap men from the Castro

No.

and take them to Reverend Gynt's place outside Reno

We have a residential treatment center there.

where they are held against their will

No, no.

while their families—from Nebraska or Idaho, or wherever you have been lecturing—pay thousands of dollars for

There are fees, of course. Residential counseling is very costly. And there's much to be gained by taking the homosexual out of the reinforcing environment, creating a different climate. But I certainly would have nothing to do with what you call kidnapping.

Reverend Gynt handles that.

No.

He requires parents to arrange it?

Frank, I simply meet the client and his family at our residential facility.

Which is over the state line.

You know, Frank, you're really making too much of this. I've had very few clients in residential counseling. That's really an insignificant part of my work.

So far. How many clients have you had actually since you began counseling gays exclusively? Or even before that?

Oh, I'm not sure of numbers.

Over a hundred?

No, not that many.

Over fifty?

No.

Less than thirty? Than twenty? Would you say that very few gays have come to avail themselves of your counseling? That your main income is lecture fees in places like Utah, where you talk to parents who are afraid their sons and daughters will run off to San Francisco? And the really fat fees might start coming from parents of gays who hire you for deprogramming?

It is true that my income is mainly earned outside the Bay Area now.

Then why do you stay here?

Well, the concerned people out there find me more credible because I live here "in

the belly of the beast,'' so to speak. Besides I love San Francisco. I hate to hear my town called the Gay Capital. I won't desert it. I must stay and counter that.

Your town?

San Francisco is my home now after five years.

My parents were born near Castro Street. So was I, almost thirty years ago, and I've been gay from as far back as I can remember. It's my town too.

Of course it is. And if you ever come for counseling, we'd end up great friends.

You think we have a lot in common?

More than you know, Frank.

One final question. Doesn't your wife work full time as a typist for an insurance company?

Yes.

How do you square that with your ideas of family life? You're not worried about confused sex roles?

I don't think there's much danger. It simply was necessary for Maxine to help out for a time, during my trial and

Didn't she hold this job before the suit?

Yes. It takes time to get established with enough clients to support a family. We came here flat broke. But she's quitting her job at the end of this month.

Because you're making more money? In fact, you've found a way to make a lot of money.

I hope so.

Well, that's about it. Thank you, Dick. And I want to assure you that this will be printed exactly as is. I won't change a word.

Thank you, Frank.

Clara finished reading the interview just as the train pulled into the Twenty-fourth Street Station. As she stood waiting for the doors to slide open, she noticed a man staring at her, probably because she had laughed aloud a couple of times while reading. She was still smiling as she stepped out of the train and looked for the escalator.

On the wall beside the moving stairway hung a pay telephone. Of course, Frank would not be home. Nevertheless, she stopped at the phone, dug a dime out of her jeans pocket, inserted it, and dialed Frank's number. Two rings, three. Four. Of course, he was out. But on the fifth ring she heard a click, a fumbling noise, a breathy pause, then, "Huh?"

"Frank?"

"Yeah?"

"Oh, good, I caught you. I couldn't wait to tell you how wonderful your interview is. I didn't expect you to be home. I was..."

"My God, what time is it?"

"Almost eleven. You sound funny. Did I wake you? You're not still sick, are you? I thought the doctor..."

"Shit! I was supposed to meet some friends down on Market Street at ten. I set the alarm, but I must have rolled over and dropped off again."

"I've just come from there. It's the first time I've ever seen the parade."

"And this is the first—no the second time I've missed it." Frank's voice had risen from a foggy, muffled tone almost to his normal, light pitch. "How is it? Big?"

"Immense. I had no idea. And I only saw a tiny bit because I have to be at the bookstore in a few minutes."

"Fun, eh."

"Hilarious. I didn't expect...it's very gay, in the old sense of the word. I expected something more political."

"It *is* political."

"Yes, of course. What I meant was...I suppose I expected a more overt statement about the assassinations of Moscone and Milk, or a..."

"That was over a year ago."

"...or more groups marching to push political programs."

"Oh, there's plenty of that in the speeches at Civic Center, but nobody stays for it. The essence of the parade is celebration, assertion, pride. That's the political statement, not the solemn, stale rhetoric your old lefty friends go in for."

Clara readied her defense of her friends, old, left, whatever. Frank would now remind her again that in the socialist countries they admired, the very existence of gay people was denied.

Then she could counter with Arthur, who was a socialist and gay, among other traits and accomplishments Frank recognized. Nevertheless Frank would reply with some dreadful quote made up on the spot and attributed to a left-wing candidate for office. It was the old ritual teasing, a dance whose steps both she and Frank knew well, a dance on the razor's edge above serious disagreement, performed in prickly challenge by Frank, while she held a more cautiously poised balance.

"You really liked the interview?" Frank was ready to skip the ritual, hurrying toward praise, asking the question with his usual slight stiffening, his gathering of forces for defense. This tone was the tribute he paid to her mind, a sign of respect and desire for her approval. She could not imagine why he should have any doubts about securing it; he was so much better at everything than she had been at his age.

"I loved it!"

Frank's sigh expressed weary pleasure. "It was a weird experience. First of all...that he was so young. I'd expect that kind of crap from someone your age, but..."

"Thanks a lot."

"You know what I mean." Frank laughed.

"Excused."

"And he was so credible. He talked and looked so calm and rational, used words and phrases borrowed from really liberal thinkers to say some absolutely crazy, murderous thing, all still rational, calm and smiling."

"That was what was so fine, the way you got under that manner and drew out the poison. You certainly had done your homework and knew just where to lead him."

"Oh, it was almost too easy. As if he felt he had outsmarted me anyway, no matter how he betrayed himself. He's not intelligent, nor educated...but there's a certain kind of cunning, you know?"

"Yes," said Clara. "He can't be all stupid, having figured out a way to make so much money."

"Which is more than I've done." Frank's voice had suddenly sharpened to its defensive edge. Clara laughed, to remind him how little she prized the ability to make money, thinking that the reminder should be unnecessary, even as she automatically responded to the edge in his voice.

"And as we talked," Frank went on, his voice loose and easy again, though not as vital as usual, "I began to have the strangest feeling. You remember when I was little and I'd get sick with a high fever, and I'd see everything getting farther and farther away—I had a bit of that feeling last week when my fever peaked—and I'd be afraid I was burning down, burning up, shriveling. . . ."

"Yes." She remembered the terrified wide eyes staring past her shoulder as he clung to her, wrapping his tiny legs and arms around her and clinging as if to retain substance by drawing her body into his.

"It was something like that, trying to talk to him. Not that I was getting smaller, but that the more clearly I saw him, revealed him, the more the distance between us grew. We were moving our lips, but so far apart, neither of us could hear a word across that abyss." Frank's solemn silence would only have been marred by any answer. "Where are you?"

"In the Twenty-fourth Street BART Station. When I drove into town I got stuck in traffic, so I put the car in a garage and watched the parade for a few minutes. No sense in taking the car out again, so I took BART down here."

"What's our schedule again?"

"I'm to read my article at the bookstore, Old Wives' Tales, stay a few minutes for questions, if any, then meet you and Arthur at Castro Gardens at one. Unless you want to meet me at Old Wives' Tales, then walk back up to Castro Street together?"

"I'd really like to. It's been a whole year, and there you are only five minutes away. But I wanted to take in some of the parade first."

"You still have time. Look, you've already seen my article, so there's no need..."

"Same one you sent me?"

"Right. And besides, who wants a mother and son reunion in the midst of a discussion group? Why don't you go and enjoy the parade, and we'll meet at the restaurant as planned."

"Good. Missed you, Mom."

The simple phrase touched her like a benediction, almost holy in its power to sooth and warm. There was no trace of the irritation of his last letter to her, nor of the coolness which had slowly eroded during the last couple of weeks of phone calls since his arrival. She could almost be glad for the week of illness which demanded her easy old maternal concern, the simple words of comfort which eased them both. "I've missed you too, dear."

"But there are these guys; we're going to the benefit show at the Castro around three. And a party after. I hope you won't feel bad if I just see you for lunch."

"No, of course not. I understand. It's a special day, and there are still lots of people you haven't seen since you got back. And you'll be a star! Everyone will be talking about your interview. It was great luck to get it into this issue. They were selling like hotcakes down at the parade. What will you do next? Another interview?"

"Hell, no. It's too much work, and it doesn't pay anything. Writing is even harder than teaching. All that work for what?"

"For the work itself, I guess," Clara murmured.

"Good old puritan Mommy."

That was the signal for another of their teasing debates, but even if there had been time, Clara would have backed off. The joy of teaching might be a sensitive subject.

"You know, this was my first time on BART. I haven't been on Twenty-fourth and Mission for about ten years. To tell the honest truth, I think the real reason I stopped to call you was to delay going up out of the station."

"What are you scared of, Mom?"

"I don't know. Not scared exactly. Just not sure what the old sights will trigger. Old memories. Old feelings."

"Don't worry. It's all different now."

"I know! How else could I be going to a *bookstore* on Valencia Street! Speaking of which, I'd better run or I'll be late. See you at one."

"Break a leg, Mom. They'll love you. It's a good article."

On the escalator, immobile as in a dream, Clara rose to brightness. The sun's rays, which had cut through the fog earlier at the parade, had spread into high noon brilliance. The sky was a cloudless, bright blue.

The corner of Twenty-fourth and Mission was transformed, opened up into a wide, red-brick expanse where BART passengers descended to trains or ascended from them. Clara tried to remember what buildings had been removed, but could not. At least one had been a bar, perhaps one a gas station. On the walls near the BART entries were murals depicting dark-skinned people dressed in bright colors, splashes of defiant pride completely different from anything she saw on these streets when she was a child. The Latinos she had known then were more like the group she saw lounging on one of the benches that curved upward, growing out of the red brick plaza.

There were four males, none of them actually sitting on the bench, but bracing against it with one foot, or leaning, or half-lying, all four of them making constant restless shuffling movements as they shifted positions. It was hard to tell their ages. They were heavy and sluggish, slumped, self-consciously sexual—that mixture Clara remembered, of old and young. She was less familiar with the type now, less able to guess whether they were still teenagers or well into their twenties. One of them, thinner than the others, had bolder eyes that moved more restlessly than his feet, darting glances at the young girls in bright dresses returning from church, crossing Mission Street with eyes fixed forward, their bodies tensed in total awareness of the intent, following male eyes. Some of the girls showed ambivalence with a blink of sultry shadowed eyelids or a swish of hips under their prim dresses as they clicked along on their high heels, but most of them stayed tight, and Clara tightened with them. Trouble. These boys, Clara decided, drawing on her memory, were distinctly the menacing type. Looking for trouble. They could have been the same boys Clara used to pass thirty-five years ago with the same nervously feigned indifference as these girls pretended. Perhaps they were the sons of those boys—more likely grandsons.

They laughed, shifted, drawled lewd comments in Spanish, then repeated them in English, not knowing that Clara understood. So, certain things about the Mission District had not changed. Angry, bored males still displayed to old women their attacks on young women. What had changed was that their laughter was even more ugly than Clara remembered.

For a moment the old, wild impatience rose up in her, the passion of her first teaching job, ironically among the toughest of these, where she found herself trying to rescue her old enemies, because she knew how these mean, frightened males would end, stunned and stunted, trapped in their shallow rebellion. Her memory-laden stare caught the eyes of the thin leader—Chico, the others called him. He looked puzzled, then hostile, then puzzled again. Clara turned away. It was too beautiful a day to worry that lives went on wasting themselves in spite of brave murals above red brick benches in bright sunlight.

She turned southward to see, a block down Mission Street, the old O'CONNOR FLORIST sign on the corner of Twenty-fifth, alone among Spanish signs, surrounded like an Irish who had foolishly wandered onto Latino territory alone. Some of the signs were Asian now too, small, with red characters. At the old florist shop Clara had ordered flowers for grandparents, in-laws, uncles, all of whom had lain in the mortuary a few doors beyond the florist before being taken to cemeteries in Daly City. She could see a bit of the mortuary jutting out beyond the florist sign. But could it be—bright yellow? Latino taste in funerals was not more colorful; if anything, more somber than Italian and Irish. What had happened? It would take only a moment to walk a block and see.

Clara passed little stores and coffee shops which had been empty, glass-front cubicles during her Depression childhood. During the war, gypsies had lived in them, beautiful dark women in long, billowing flower-print skirts, appearing for a year or two and then suddenly gone, like short-lived butterflies. After the war, the street had not done much better, as prosperous workers moved to the suburbs. She recognized one more old store, another survivor selling mirrors and glass.

Then, crossing Twenty-fifth Street, she saw why the funeral home had been painted bright yellow. A great sign proclaimed it THE MISSION CHILD CARE CONSORTIUM. No longer a house of death, but of new life. So the poor were no longer putting so much money into death.

Facing it from the other side of Mission Street was another astonishing sign, MISSION CULTURAL CENTER, on a huge building Clara recognized as an old furniture store, its display windows darkened, its facade dingy. She looked through one of the glass doors, pushed at it tentatively. It swung open and she walked in. In the middle of the vast showroom rose a small stage surrounded by seats for an audience. She wandered past the darkened stage, through dim silence to a stairway, which took her up to a well-lit gallery hung with bright paintings, mostly of rural South American subjects, in primitive or poster style. She walked around the gallery twice before going downstairs and out of the quiet place, noting that a concert was scheduled for next week. As she came out onto the street, she was smiling. It was not the quality of the paintings as art that cheered her. They expressed the need to express, the joy in making that lifted the heart of the maker and, therefore, lifted Clara's heart too, made her brave enough to lift her head toward Army Street, lift her eyes to the hill beyond.

Her eyes fastened on one particular row of houses on one particular street rimming the low slope. She could see only the upper edges, like a row of false teeth between the rows of more irregular peaked-roofed houses climbing the hill. The grassy mound at the top of Bernal Heights was still bare as it had been when Clara used to climb up to sit in the quiet, alone, beneath the air raid siren installed after Pearl Harbor.

Just before Clara and the Great Depression were born, a developer had strung the stucco cubes, twenty of them, along the low ridge, then had gone broke. The houses went up for sale just after the stockmarket crash, bought and lost by owners whose jobs and hopes crashed, prices falling and again falling until Clara's parents were able to meet the down payment on one. Clara was just starting to walk when they moved in.

Her first memory was of the treacherously slick, triply waxed hardwood floors on which she could not keep to her unsteady feet. Not that she was allowed any practice. These precious floors were destined for constant polishing, later for covering with rugs, neither of which were to be stepped upon more than necessary. Clara and her parents were shut into the kitchen. There Clara ate, read, did her homework. There her parents counted the money earned in their shop. The silence among them was filled by the voices of radio or by the movies to which they escaped from each other, together.

Except for sleeping and bathing, Clara was allowed to enter the other rooms only to share her mother's rigid routine of daily cleaning, or for monthly family gatherings, preceded and followed by a further fury of cleaning and polishing. The fireplace in the small living room had never held a fire, its pale bricks remaining creamy throughout the forty years her parents lived there.

The view across the Mission rooftops (not quite to the bridges or the Bay, since the street barely rose above Army Street) could be seen only from a small window in Clara's bedroom. During long, fevered afternoons of illness, when all fearsome rules against using, soiling, rumpling, were suspended, Clara lay in bed looking at the vista of peaked roofs jutting into the sky, revealed by the narrow opening. Often sick, her parents at their shop, she could lie in the luxury of unwatched silence, surrounded by library books scattered on the bed.

The new owners (Frank had boldly gone to see and had reported to her) moved the living room to the view side, adding another fireplace. As Clara looked up, she thought she could see the flash of reflecting sun on the huge window with which they had opened up the wall of her bedroom. But maybe she only imagined that, as she imagined them opening all the doors, uncovering the floors, walking on them wherever they pleased, rumpling their bedspreads, lounging on a living room sofa, blackening the fireplace with roaring flames which would remove forever from that house the chill of fear, the incapacity for joy.

When Clara was eighteen, impending marriage hanging over her like an enchantment no prince came to break, the widower down the street finally succeeded in drinking himself to death. His house came on the market at a good price. Dino's parents put a small downpayment on it, presenting the deed and the mortgage to Dino and Clara on their wedding day. Like a sleepwalker, Clara moved half a block away, into a house identical to her parents' house, except that its precious hardwood floors were stained and scratched, and remained so. Those floors were Clara's mild rebellion, along with her insistence on finishing State College though pregnant, and on teaching though she had a child.

It had taken ten more years of small, fearful rebellions mixed with steadfast, exhausting conformities to split Clara's life wide open, forcing her escape from Dino, her family, The City itself. For another ten years she made brief monthly visits to her parents' kitchen, and endured holiday family gatherings for Frank's sake. She was relieved when her parents moved to a fenced, guarded retirement community on the south peninsula. There they lived as always, huddled beside a television set, counting their now considerable money, their fear of losing it or using their house stronger than ever. By then Frank was old enough to attend family gatherings without her, and her infrequent visits to her parents no longer took her through the old streets of the Mission. Even when Frank moved back to The City after college, she never visited him here. He preferred to spend an occasional weekend with her up in Ukiah or to meet her in a restaurant in North Beach or on Clement Street, as Arthur and her other old friends did.

But now, standing safely between the MISSION CHILD CARE CONSORTIUM and the MISSION CULTURAL CENTER, Clara could look up at that old row of stucco cubes without blinking. As she turned her back on them and began retracing her steps, she slipped into an unassailably good memory of walking up Mission Street, alone as a child and later with Frank running along beside her, telling all passersby that he was "going to the library!" His articulation, even at three, was already so clear and precise that he never passed through the stage of calling it the "libary."

Reaching Twenty-fourth Street again, Clara ignored the male foursome, still posturing and growling, now openly passing a bottle and some white tablets among them. As she turned left, up Twenty-fourth, the feeling of expansion came just as it always had when she reached the last block before her marble refuge, palace, fortress: Public Library—Mission Branch. It was a small, two-storey box, covering no more space than the store on the opposite corner, but in her imagination it always rose and spread to cover at least a whole block, and its walls, bare except for the names of authors etched in the marble, somehow sprouted statues of those demigods, visible only to her eyes, rising to gigantic size, their heads in the sky:

TOLSTOY	DICKENS
HUGO	SCOTT
DUMAS	THACKERAY
HAWTHORNE	POE
BALZAC	MARK TWAIN
GEORGE ELIOT	IRVING

She found she could still recite the lists, even the one hidden on the west side of the building:

LOWELL
BRYANT
WHITTIER
HOLMES
LONGFELLOW
EMERSON

One day, when she was about twelve, she had met an old man for whom she copied the lists because he was too nearsighted to read the walls. He told her he was a member of the Order of Masons, and that he believed the lists of authors comprised a code by which the architect had left a secret message. Almost every time she came to the library she saw him sitting at a corner table near the reference books, arranging and rearranging the letters of the great names. She wondered if he had ever cracked the code, but was never intensely curious. The names as they were held sufficient magic for her.

She hurried past the library, turning right at Valencia Street. The jumble of shabby shops and bars crowding the next three blocks included a crowded coffee house and two bookstores she would have visited, had there been time. Near the corner of Twenty-first Street she read OLD WIVES' TALES gracefully painted across a narrow shop window. Taped to the window was a sheet of paper announcing MARATHON GAY FREEDOM DAY READINGS. Her name was first on the list under the title. As she pushed open the door, she confronted rows of bookcases which had been pushed up to the front of the store. She recognized the woman standing between a bookcase and the small counter. "Hi, Marge."

"Clara! Just in time." The woman hugged her, then drew her past the bookcases to the space which had been cleared in the back of the store. At least forty women and a few men were crowded into the space, some sitting on the few chairs but most huddled on the floor. Four more women, who had been browsing at bookshelves on the walls, followed Clara and Marge, squeezing into the crowd.

"How long has it been?" Clara asked, pulling back from Marge and peering at her long face.

"Two years? Almost three."

"You look wonderful," Clara said. She did. Her tan-gold hair had grown longer and spikier, her face thinner. Marge was one of those pale women who look younger and frailer as their strength and energy increase. She grinned, hugged Clara again, then turned to the audience.

It was a young group. Except for a white-haired woman seated on one of the few chairs, and a couple about Clara's age, everyone appeared to be under thirty. A few even looked under twenty. Nearly all were white and fair-haired. Marge had explained to Clara that the readings at the store drew many newcomers to the Bay Area, often from mid-American states. In the summer especially, the store drew visitors from everywhere. She could not guarantee a large audience on Gay Freedom Day, but those who left the parade and street fair to hear some of the readings were sure to be receptive and serious.

"Let's get started." She waited for quiet. "I'm Marge Raven, and I work here. As you know, we're having a marathon reading to celebrate publication of *Strong Talk,* the new anthology of articles by women, which I edited along with Ailey Laster, who's over there, up front by the counter." A small, dark woman, her features indistinguishable because of the strong light coming through the store windows behind her, nodded at the smatter of applause. "If you stick around all day, you'll hear and meet seven of the women represented in this book, each of whom will read her article or story and answer some questions.

"Our first reader is Clara Lontana, professor of history at Mendocino State University near Ukiah. Doctor Lontana—Clara—has been at Mendo State for twelve years, since 1968. In 1974 she started women's studies classes there. She has been active in community projects, including the Battered Women Shelter and the Northwoods Alcohol and Drug Abuse Program. Her articles on immigrant women have been published in several scholarly journals, and she is working on a history of female immigrant labor in the United States.

"Clara Lontana has been granted several honors. I'll just name two of them. In 1977 she was voted teacher of the year by Mendo State students. In 1979 she was named 'the greatest threat to American values' by the Newsletter of the God and

43

Country Association of Northern California." A surge of laughter and applause rose. Marge joined the laughter, then waited for it to die down. "She has just been elected head of the History Department of Mendo State, which proves something."

"It proves," said Clara, "that I wasn't smart enough to dodge that tedious and powerless honor." More laughter, softer but warm. Clara sensed the group's good will, their eagerness to like her reading. She only hoped they would not be disappointed; her article was, after all, very serious, and more personal than she would ordinarily write.

"Not to prolong this introduction, but I have to tell you how I happen to be making it, how we got Clara to write a piece for our book, how we got her down here today." She took Clara's hand, squeezed it, then held it as she went on. "I was born and raised in Ukiah, and when I went to Mendo State, I was lucky enough to get into a class taught by Clara. I won't bore you with the details of how she inspired me, how she goes after all her students, demanding that they be the best they can. . .that we all become ourselves. I'll just say it was partly because of Clara that I found the courage to come out as a lesbian, to leave Ukiah, to start building my own real life."

Clara kept smiling, but inwardly she winced. Praise from students was sweet if only it would stop at calling a specific job well done. She felt uncomfortable when they handed her the credit for life choices which she often viewed with surprise, and sometimes with dismay. She always wondered how they felt when problems arose out of these choices. Did they then blame her as they had praised her?

"So now I'll stop talking and just let Clara read her essay." She let go of Clara's hand. "Clara Lontana, sharing her unique perspective on the assassination of George Moscone and Harvey Milk."

MURDER IN SAN FRANCISCO

I was born in San Francisco's Mission District in 1930, the only child of parents born in Italy. In those days, although people used neighborhood names like Noe Valley, Eureka Valley, Bernal Heights, and Potrero Hill, these were all considered parts of the basin bounded by three hills and by Market Street, called the Mission District. South of Bernal Heights lay the Outer Mission, encompassing areas with names like Excelsior and Crocker Amazon.

The Mission District had traditionally been a settlement of mixed European immigrant working class families, who generally moved out when they prospered, making room for new immigrants. When I was born, there was a bare sprinkling of old Nordic immigrants left. The larger population was Irish and Italian. By the time I entered Mission High, at the end of World War Two, the new wave of immigrants came from the Western Hemisphere. Hispanics poured into the Mission, bordered by blacks in the Fillmore and Bayview-Hunters Point.

The Mission District was very different in the thirties and forties from what it is now. No television: families went to the movies, three double features a week, even in the depths of the Depression. I saw books in school and at the public library, never in anyone's home, nor in a store. I never saw a political poster beyond the level of ZAP THE JAPS! The adults I knew, except my teachers, had little schooling. Few of my classmates cared about learning in high school, let alone going beyond. By the time I was in high school, I was making my trips to the library alone, hiding my books and report cards. My public life consisted of "going steady" with a son of immigrants similar to my family and perfecting my jitterbug style.

I felt like a thinly disguised alien, living in constant fear of exposure to ridicule and hatred, vaguely threatened by the ever-present danger of being ground up by a machine into which I could not fit, hard as I (to my shame) tried. No doubt there were others like me, but we never found each other, so intent were we on masquerading as assembly-line parts of the machine.

The way the machine worked can best be explained by describing the career of one of my classmates, whom I will call Richie. Richie had an Italian mother and an Irish father, and was an altar boy at Saint Anthony's. I first knew him in fifth grade, when our teacher asked me to help him with his reading. Richie was not at all disturbed by his inability to read, and I soon grew impatient with his cheerful assumption that if he waited long enough I would read the words for him. My job was taken over by Alicia, who kept it for the rest of her life.

At Mission High Richie played football and Alicia was a cheerleader. Envy of Richie's athletic feats was never a threat to his popularity because these feats were balanced by his amiable dullness and minor sins. He cheated clumsily on exams, was just sufficiently drunk at school dances, and smiled when asked if he had been hit on the head too many times during football practice.

Only one old-maid English teacher ever said a word against Richie. She told me I would "go far" while Richie would be lucky to get a job as a milkman. She was wrong on several counts. Supermarkets put an end to home-delivered milk; and Richie went through college on football scholarships, becoming a high school football coach, then rapidly rising to administrative positions. Along the way he married Alicia and they moved out to the Avenues.

The next time I encountered Richie, he was sitting on the board which interviewed me when I applied for a job teaching in the public schools. Working through college while having a son, I completed my studies two years after Richie. During the interview, he was the one who mentioned my son, asking if I believed a mother could or should be a good teacher. In 1954 his question was rhetorical; it was clear that the seven male faces surveying me thought not. I don't remember what I answered. Richie asked about my husband, who had played football with him, and brought me best regards from Alicia, who was happily in her third pregnancy, glad to be done with the office jobs in which she had helped him through college, home for good. This hint, about the proper use of a wife's mind, was common in those times.

Despite Richie's objection, my civil service exam and recommendations prevailed, and I was hired. I was assigned to Continuation High School, the place where that old English teacher used to threaten Richie he would end up if he continued to shirk homework and cheat on exams. I don't know how much Richie had to do with that particular irony.

During the next few years I saw many other Richies moving into positions of power in all branches of civil service and city government, almost automatically, like standardized parts which fit smoothly into the machine. The standardized features became clear: male, Catholic, white, formerly athletic, and, above all, mediocre. These men were quite comfortable with inefficiency or corruption, but terrified by ideas. Time after time I saw or experienced senseless obstacles used to frustrate good work. Even so, it was a long time before I could comprehend the extent of the hatred and fear of competency, of intelligence, of anything but the low cunning that played the game and held a place in a machine which had to be kept safe for one's own kind.

I do not mean to say that no competent or talented people worked in civil service jobs in San Francisco. There were many, but much of their energy was wasted in confronting obstacles created by the Richies in power. Nor were minorities and women totally barred from jobs, but those who advanced tended to fit the mold of fearful mediocrity: Richie again, under the skin.

Am I only describing the pattern of vested interests in most cities? That is a valid question, but one which belongs in another discussion than this one.

At any rate, in 1960 I moved to Berkeley to do graduate work, and then to teach on a college campus in the north woods. This move was, for personal reasons, the right and necessary one for me, a part of important changes in my life. The courage to make these changes grew with the help of another group of immigrants who began coming to San Francisco in the fifties.

They came from the east, mostly New Yorkers, often Jews, well-read and incorrigibly verbal, intense, quick. Some of them were ducking the FBI and they loved me because I hadn't enough political sense to be afraid to be their friend. I loved them because they hadn't the sense to see that Richie and his kind were invincibly, permanently in power. They laughed at Richie, mimicked his illiterate pronouncements, fought him, and each time they lost, laughed again and began to prepare for the next battle. They were people who had always lived in a big city. Not only street smart, they were meeting smart, board smart, election smart. Their laughter was part of their stamina. Each time they laughed at a "Richie" or argued with me, they increased my courage. In 1960, when two of them were called to City Hall for harassment by the Un-American Activities Committee, I joined in the picket lines of support for them. I knew by name all the guards who kept us out of the hearing room. I had gone to school with the policemen who turned the hoses on us; one of them was my brother-in-law.

Though I left San Francisco at that point, others like me, both immigrants and natives, did not. Their numbers increased. Whatever the convulsions of the sixties did or failed to do, they did somehow give birth to the women's movement and gay movement of the seventies. Though by that time I was teaching in the rural north, I had a strong stake in both movements, as a woman and as the mother of a gay man.

When my son finished college and returned to San Francisco in 1972, I knew that he was returning to a city different from the one we had left twelve years before. Although he eventually decided to settle elsewhere, I was grateful that he was back home in San Francisco while it was the center of a movement that would help him grow into self-acceptance sooner than I had. For in his way he had, like me, always lived in disguise, a misfit in constant fear of exposure and rejection.

Although this introduction may seem purely personal, I hope that I can show its relevancy to the murder of George Moscone and Harvey Milk by Dan White. It has been said that Dan White is a classic homophobe, and that he killed Harvey Milk because Milk was gay. His murder of George Moscone is explained by Moscone's refusal to reinstate White after a too hasty resignation. All this may be true, but it is part of a larger historical picture which I have tried to sketch with parts of my personal experience. Let us consider how these three men, assassin and victims, fit into this picture.

George Moscone, like my schoolmate Richie, was born in 1929, also a native San Franciscan, Italian, Catholic. He attended Catholic schools and was a basketball star—at strongly academic Saint Ignatius High School. Moscone went through College of Pacific on an athletic scholarship, but then won an academic scholarship to Hastings Law School. In other words, despite his superficial similarity to Richie, Moscone showed signs of the misfit: he was clearly not a mediocre intellect. Such men traditionally (like those other slightly misfit people, the native Jews of San Francisco) stayed out of city government and civil service, excelling in business and the professions, coexisting in peace with the unthreatened Richies. In the ordinary course of things, Moscone would have made a good income in private practice, then might have nurtured his broader community interests by support of local arts and charities. But the changing times and population had created a constituency for him. His time had come. He moved gracefully through successful terms as supervisor, then state senator, until in 1975, for the first time in The City's history as I know it, San Francisco elected a bright, innovative, liberal, literate mayor.

Harvey Milk was the same age as Moscone. He had graduated from college too, but was not so good an athlete nor a scholar as Moscone. And, of course, Milk was no ethnic, Catholic native. He was one of the new immigrants, a New York Jew, like the quick, abrasive friends who had taught me to laugh at Richie and had been fighting him ever since the fifties. Milk had arrived late, in 1969. Moreover, he was a politically conservative financial analyst when he came. But he was quickly transformed into an anti-war, liberal, avowedly gay fighter with courage and stamina. He set out to learn and to use the political process in order to make change. It was on his fourth try at public office, in 1977, that he won his seat as supervisor.

Dan White was born eighteen years after Moscone and Milk. Reared in the Outer Mission in an Irish Catholic family, he attended Catholic elementary schools and public high school, where he tested "average" and was an enthusiastic athlete. After high school he did a few months at City College and a hitch in the army. Perhaps he was never offered an athletic scholarship to college. By the time Dan White was in high school, these scholarships were less sure to be awarded for athletic prowess, more being given on the basis of minority status. If so, this must have been his first encounter with a hitch in the machine he was supposed to fit into. After the army White spent a couple of years in and out of both the police and fire departments, then started an ill-fated business, a fast food concession.

My guess is that, if events had not intervened, he would have quietly dumped his failing business and settled for a place back in the police department where he still had many friends. The machine still worked well enough to place him there, though it could no longer be counted on to raise him to a powerful position.

It is ironic that the liberals' successful fight for district elections of supervisors not only made it possible for Harvey Milk to be elected by liberal and gay support, but made it possible for Dan White to be elected by a constituency who chose the young White almost as a throwback to earlier ways of power in The City. The simultaneous election of two such opposites is often cited as evidence of "polarization" of The City, but that term is misleading. It implies that before 1977 there had been consensus or compromise among disagreeing factions. No such compromise was or ever had been possible. Until Moscone's victory, the liberal and competent simply had no power, no chance to make change. Now they existed and voted in sufficient numbers to indicate glimmerings of the beginning of power. In other words, polarization had always existed. It now became evident because the formerly silenced could make themselves heard.

They were clearly heard in the voices of Milk, Moscone, and Supervisor Silver. Though not a majority, the liberals were clearly a force, an influence, and for many, an exciting hope. For Dan White, they must have been an infuriating harassment, suffered like a thousand thrusts of rapier wit, at his expense. In every exchange between them and him, he was out-thought, out-talked, out-witted. I think of Richie, who did not care that I could read and he could not—because he knew from the beginning that in the long run he would rule me. But Dan White had no such certainty. He had been born twenty years too late. The rules of the game had changed, and he lacked the necessary components to succeed by the new ones. Like City College, the police department, the fire department, his failing business, he had hit another dead end. He responded as he had to earlier frustration: he quit, on November 10, 1978, less than a year after taking office. For once, his decision to quit was probably the right one, but he quit that too, asking to be reinstated five days later.

Of course, Moscone should have reinstated him. In the horror of what happened it is too easy to forget that White was elected by his district and that a hasty decision, quickly withdrawn, is a permissible mistake. But political reality prevailed. With the power to appoint a replacement, Moscone could add another liberal to the board and intended to do so. White must have known when he turned in his resignation that that was exactly what Moscone would do.

Why did White reverse himself and demand to be reinstated? He is quoted as saying that supporters stepped forward to offer him help. No doubt they did. No doubt many people told him he stood for something of great value to them. I can imagine the vehemence with which his constituency urged him to withdraw his resignation. I can imagine with what inflammatory and violent anti-gay, anti-semitic, macho, anti-intellectual obscenities some of the egged him on. I can imagine, because I grew up on all their phrases. I often wonder if any of White's close supporters have lost sleep pondering their role, their words, in creating Dan White, a living embodiment of their casually voiced pride in stupidity, cruelty, and fear.

If you consider this a harsh judgment of White's constituency, if you question my portrait of White as representative of an old power machine now threatened by liberals, minorities, women: consider the verdict at Dan White's trial in May, 1979—voluntary manslaughter, maximum sentence seven years. This, for a man who, when refused reinstatement, shot down the mayor in his own office, then while Moscone lay on the floor, fired two more shots into his head; a man who remained sufficiently composed to reload his gun, then go to the office of Supervisor Harvey Milk and repeat this act with five more bullets.

Members of this jury wept openly for Dan White. He was one of theirs, a martyr to old San Francisco, to things as they had been. I heard of the verdict from 200 miles away. My son, I am glad to say, was four times that distance, having left only a few days before, luckily. For if he had been in the city of his birth, he might have become caught up in the outrage which exploded in riots near City Hall, as he saw the way in which his mother's old enemies had become his own literally deadly enemies.

The death of Moscone and Milk was a tragedy. The jury's verdict was a disgrace capping a long history of invisible, mean-spirited little murders which preceded these two open assassinations. But at least it was open murder, public disgrace, watched with horror by the whole world. Not only gays are out of the closet. The Richies of San Francisco have come out from behind their amiable masks and have been exposed for the killers they are.

The clapping began tentatively, then grew louder and remained steady. No one was smiling at Clara now. They all looked at her intently, almost fervently. She could not have won an audience more completely. She was surprised. This was easier than reading a paper at a conference of her colleagues. Easier than teaching—hit and run, with no papers to take home and read.

The applause stopped suddenly. After a moment of utter silence, Marge, now seated on the floor against the wall, waved an arm. "I think there's time for a few questions." Silence. Then a voice from a small, freckled girl in the front row. "If my parents were like you, I'd still be in Arkansas." Laughter shook the group out of their solemnity, and several hands went up. Clara nodded at a solitary young man in the back, hunched up against a bookcase.

"You mentioned that your son left San Francisco. Where is he and what is he doing?"

"At the time I wrote this article—right after the trial—my son was in Canada, teaching in a private high school. He returned to San Francisco last month." She hesitated, blocked by the thought of Frank's reasons for returning. Of course, no one had asked her for his reasons. But she found herself rushing ahead, changing the subject. "Actually I'm on my way to see him when I leave here. He is the Frank Lontana who did the interview in that copy of *Gay Streets* you're holding." Clara smiled proudly at the applause for Frank. Yet she felt vaguely uncomfortable, as if she had evaded the man's real question.

A black girl with braided hair, her voice almost a whisper, spoke from Clara's right. "How did you find out your son was gay?"

"He told me," said Clara. "In 1965, when he was fifteen. He said that for a couple of years he had been testing everyone, making references to homosexuality and watching for snickers or hostility. He said I was the only person he knew who had passed his test." Again Clara felt as if the rest of her answer were cut off at her throat, leaving them with a false impression of her as an ideal mother, free of all prejudice. Surely she was proud to have been the parent to whom a boy turned with his secret, but would this group appreciate the irony of the "prize" Frank had awarded her for passing his test?

"How did you feel when he told you?" The question came from the white-haired lady, who did have something like a spark of irony in her eyes.

"Scared. Guilty." Clara hesitated, sighed, hesitated again. "I don't mean to give such abrupt answers, but...it's very hard to convey what it was like. Like a mixture of all emotions—love, fear, anger—you name it, all mixed up, but mostly fear. Let me just say that, at that time, I never dreamed that within fifteen years I'd be discussing this openly, in public, for a sympathetic audience...if that gives you any idea of how it felt at the time."

"Isolated," murmured the white-haired lady.

"Like your son," said the man who held the copy of *Gay Streets*.

"And that must have been partly what brought you and your son close together," added Marge. It was not a question. If it had been, Clara would not have known how to answer it. She and Frank had not marched hand in hand through his teens, smiling, like the mother and child in the parade. She supposed they had had the normal problems, complicated by divorce, political upheaval, and Frank's secret.

"How long before he came out?"

"Three or four years later, when he was at UCLA, he wrote a letter to *Time Magazine*, protesting a slur on homosexuals, signing his name and address. That was his coming out gesture. I remember they called him before printing it, to make sure he really wanted them to print his full name and address. He was very sure, quite deliberate. He got a lot of letters, started a gay group at UCLA, was very active from then on."

A girl in overalls, who looked about sixteen, raised her hand. "How did his father react? Did you really keep your son's secret from him all that time?"

"Oh. My article skips over my marital status, doesn't it? I married the nice Italian boy down the street. We divorced in 1960 when I left The City. He remarried and moved to L.A., where Frank visits him from time to time. I've had no contact with him for over fifteen years, so I can't say what his attitude is."

Clara felt the slight heat of a flush that still passed through her whenever she told a lie. Even a small lie. In fact, Frank had reported to her that Dino had taken the news with an almost casual dismissal of it. "Now that you're away from *her*, you'll be all right, you'll meet some nice girl and fall in love and get married." She could win more sympathy from this group, making Dino appear very stupid, by simply quoting him. But, as a matter of fact, his simplistic and cruel answer had not been so very different from the accepted opinion of psychologists at the time. Nor had one of Clara's faint, unvoiced hopes been so very different from Dino's opinion: that Frank's homosexuality might be a passing "phase." In any case, she really had no idea what thought processes Dino had gone through when no nice girl changed Frank's preference.

"Was your husband a 'Richie'?" asked a voice from the side wall.

No. Yes. Dino could have been, but not without Clara's energy, not without her desire to create and support and be wife to a Richie. Or did Dino want...oh, it was so long ago. "Richie is a type. People are not just types. They are more complex. Perhaps it is a weakness of my article...." Clara felt the faint trickle of sweat that sometimes tickled her back on hot September days in the classroom. But this sweat was not caused by heat; it came from the strain of peering through the tangle of memory and trying to select pieces of truth that did not become lies when taken out of their context, their time. In a classroom Clara was expert at orchestrating a discussion, eliciting the questions which illuminated broad issues. There she could provide facts gleaned from long and continuing study. She had not expected it to be more difficult to extract the truth from her own experience.

"Your article mentioned the importance of being Catholic," said a pink-cheeked girl with an almost classic Irish pug nose and blue eyes. "I assume you were raised Catholic. It must have been hard to break free of that."

No. Yes. "There are all sorts of Catholics. Some who practiced birth control, even back then, went to church only to observe birth, marriage, death, and Christmas. Many Italians were like that. My family too. In fact, when I saw the 'sisters' in the parade today, they reminded me of the nuns who used to wait for me after school, trying to get me to go to church. My parents shunned them the same as I did.''

At that moment there was a commotion near the front of the store. Clara looked and saw a flash of green and then—yes, it was the old woman she had seen ranting at the parade. She was babbling something and shaking a finger as a woman came from behind the counter and gently led her out of the store. ''That's only Myrtle,'' Marge said softly. ''Lives in a half-way house on Sixteenth. Between trips to the state hospital. She has lucid days when she's really nice. We try to look out for her.''

''So you got some of your liberal ideas from your parents?''

Clara looked back at the earnest Irish girl, paused, then shook her head. Sometimes she thought the only thing she had escaped was the comfort of confession, the hope of candle lighting. Otherwise her home had been as full of inhibition and fear as any strictly Catholic home of those days. ''No, in other things, my parents are quite conservative.''

''Then you had to make a real break with your family too. I mean, divorce and all, in your family, twenty years ago, that must have been almost like telling them you were gay.''

No. Yes? Divorce and desertion were not completely unknown to Clara's family. Divorce as a solution to drinking, gambling, infidelity, beating, was acceptable—a tragedy but not a disgrace. It was Clara's reasons for divorce that were disgraceful; it was her divorce from her family's expectations and values, from the family itself, that was abominable. Yes. Clara felt she could nod honestly to this question. Yes. Divorce for her reasons had been as mysterious and repugnant to her family as Frank's later announcement that he was gay.

Silence. They were waiting for her to say something. The young people in this audience were not satisfied with a simple nod to this question. They were fresh in their anger at their parents' opposition and rejection. They wanted Clara to articulate and legitimize that anger. They wanted her to tell them she had made a clean break with her family and created a new, better life for herself. Yes. No. It was, again, more complex than she had time to explain. Would they understand? Perhaps it could not be explained, but could only be lived.

If she tried to give them the whole truth and if they could understand it, they would not like what they learned. She would have to tell them that, unless they were very lucky, they were in for something more painful than the clear anger they now felt. When anger has evaporated, she would say, and parents grow old and sick and fragile, then comes the real pain. Then they wait for your phone calls, your brief, formal visits, still abhorring everything that you have become. Worst of all, you realize that, hating and craving you as they do, they also love you, and they are trying their best. They are trying as hard as you are, harder, since their perception is so narrow, yet wide enough to see that they fail, try and fail, as you do. And the pain of it makes you stammer that you love them, then increases as you realize you really do.

"Your family hasn't ever...the break never...." The Irish girl seemed to have read her mind, perhaps because something in her struggle paralleled Clara's. There were tears in her eyes as she let her question hang, unasked.

Clara decided that her own truth need not be everyone's. "I've known people whose parents have come around. So don't stop trying. Things change. People change."

"But your article says people haven't changed," said the young man in the back row. "It says the murderers, the Richies of this town are still here, still in power, ready to destroy us." His voice quivered slightly and cracked on the last word.

"Yes," said Clara, grateful that someone had finally returned to her article, "but the circumstances have changed.

60

Remember, I said the violence is exposed, which in itself means a shift of power. And all of you are here now." Clara smiled. She had seen her opportunity to make a happy conclusion and escape. "That means everything is different. The Mission can never go back to what it was before." She turned to glance at Marge, who took her hint.

"On that note," Marge stood and took Clara's hand again, "we'll thank Clara Lontana and let her go to meet her son."

The applause pursued Clara through the store and out into the street.

"Did we have to meet here?" Arthur was clearly in one of his more acid moods. His wide mouth thinned into a hard line cutting through his trim beard, which had remained black as the hair on his head had gradually grayed and thinned. He squinted as if resenting the bright sun shining on him and Clara as they sat in the back garden of the restaurant, hidden from the noisy parade pouring out to its conclusion on Castro Street.

"It's near Frank."

"Don't tell me he's living in the Castro again." His eyes swept over the waiters briskly moving around the tables. Young, slim men in tight jeans with striped T-shirts, tightly shorn hair and small moustaches, they smiled and joked as they passed each other. Arthur did not smile.

"He's renting a room in someone's house until he finds a place of his own."

"I can find him something cheaper and better across town. What's he want to come back here for?"

"Well, it's his home, the place where he was born."

Arthur gave Clara what Frank used to call his laser look, a continuous piercing glare. "This is most certainly not the place where he was born."

"Not anymore, thank God," Clara laughed. "This place was a boarded-up old cigar store when he was little."

Arthur's eyes darted about until they impaled one of the waiters from whom he firmly requested and obtained tea and water for two, menus for three. When he was younger, Arthur seemed irritably shrill in his intolerance of things Clara tended to put up with. Now his nervous irritability had matured into a certain authority. Clara had years ago learned that his abrasive manner was part of an unfailing integrity and a sturdy generosity, gaining weight as his once-skeletal body had in middle age.

"I know," she said. "You had a terrible time parking, then had to push your way through crowds to get here. Frank is late, you're hungry, the service is slow. . . ."

"Inconveniences which make you glow with euphoria."

"This is the first time I've walked through the old neighborhood since I left it. Do you know how many bookstores there are between here and Mission Street?"

"I'm sure you'll tell me." He pushed aside a tendril of ivy that touched his ear, then pursed his lips into a kind if mocking smile, nodding as Clara began to describe her tour.

Twenty years ago, when Clara moved to Berkeley, she was sent to Arthur by friends who had picketed City Hall with her. Arthur held the lease on a large south campus house and was willing to sublet rooms to her and Frank. He was thirty in 1960, the same age as Clara. He hardly spoke to her, and never to Frank, except to warn them about the piano, which she and Frank must never touch, but which Arthur was quite likely to play at all hours, especially the predawn ones.

After their first week, he spoke to Clara again, to tell her she was not to wash his dishes along with her own, and that, in any case, Frank should do all the dishes. Somehow, within the next few weeks, Clara discovered Frank with Arthur at the piano, receiving a music lesson. The "bright brat," as

Arthur called him, progressed so fast that he was allowed the piano, during prescribed hours, with carefully washed hands.

Arthur and Clara began to walk to the campus together, gradually telling each other about themselves. Although demonstrations had ended the City Hall hearings, Arthur had lost his teaching job in Fremont when the newspapers listed him among those subpoenaed. He saw no point in going back to New York, where his totally left-wing ancestry was even better known, and where relatives were always producing another nice socialist girl for him. He had saved enough money to keep him through completion of his M.A. in music. After that, it was probably hand-to-mouth private teaching for him.

Though nervous and sharp-tongued, he was entirely without self-pity or meanness, surprisingly easy to live with. He exploded in genuine anger only once, when, on a bad day, Clara said she had probably made a mistake and ought to go back to Dino. Arthur had nodded politely at Dino when he came ostensibly to visit Frank, actually to hang around Clara, but had never otherwise mentioned Dino. Now he raged, screamed at Clara, "That man is your death!" and threatened to throw her out should she ever "start sniveling again." His suddenly exposed horror of Dino was more bracing than his words. She always remembered Arthur's tantrum with gratitude.

Nevertheless, within the year, Clara found a small apartment for herself and Frank. The gamelan and sitar were all right, Clara said; it was the bassoon at 4 a.m. that drove her out. By that time their friendship was formed. They ate together at least twice a week. They went to concerts, sometimes performed or conducted by Arthur, sometimes by others performing Arthur's compositions while he sat in sweat-drenched agony, Clara holding his hand. This close contact continued until 1968, when Clara went to Ukiah and Frank went to UCLA.

Arthur moved to San Francisco where he taught private students at home and classes at the Jewish Community Center. Despite his irritability, children liked him as Frank had, and he soon had many students. In 1971 he inherited some money with which he bought a big old house near the Center. He rented rooms to a few music students, beginning almost by accident to coach them in school subjects which suffered because of music practice and performance. By 1975 Arthur's house had become the JSB School (after J. S. Bach) for ages ten to eighteen, teaching all subjects to serious young musicians who needed a study schedule outside what traditional schools demanded. Except for an occasional lab course at Galileo High School, his forty to sixty students were taught by Arthur and his two full-time and several part-time teachers. A dozen or so students lived at the school, sent from some distance as the reputation of the school grew. There was now a waiting list, and the *Chronicle* regularly called asking to do a feature story, which Arthur regularly and rudely refused to allow.

"...and I even walked by Mission High. Someone had spray-painted the west wall, on Church Street, U.S. OUT OF EL SALVADOR."

"A superior form of vandalism?"

"Better than FUCK YOU, which is all I ever saw when I went to school there."

"A question of interpretation," Arthur insisted. "You seem to interpret all this..." The rest of Arthur's sentence was drowned out by a blast from the marching band, swept by the wind over the intervening buildings to the garden. Arthur frowned. "...instead of more sound and fury, signifying..." He snapped a hand shut, a conductor's cut-off, as if to silence the music from the street. "...nothing!"

"I disagree! You know you don't mean that. The bigger the crowds, the louder and sillier they are, the less shame and fear and danger Frank—and you—will live with, until there's none at all for gay people, and then all this will disappear."

"What if it should turn out that the bigger the parade, the worse off we are?"

Clara shook her head. "You used to march in the Gay Freedom Day Parade, starting with the very first one."

"No more. I refuse to be part of a commercial for baths, bars and boutiques."

"Oh, Arthur, don't be such an old-time queer! You can't dismiss all this so easily. We've known each other for twenty years, lived together, shared our troubles. You got me through the divorce. For eight years we saw each other at least twice a week..."

"What has all that got to do with..."

"...and in all that time, you never talked about being gay, never had a lover in the house when I lived there."

"I was between lovers at the time."

"You know what I mean. We were the closest of friends, yet your love life was unmentionable. I told you about the men I was seeing, but you never told me. All those silly antics out there in the street..." Clara waved her hand, and a muffled cheer rose, ending the music, as if she had finally cut it off. "All that is putting an end to silence and...well...for the sake of my son, I'm grateful." Clara leaned back and waited for Arthur's counterattack, but he only eyed her thoughtfully, then turned toward a hovering waiter, whose partially unbuttoned fly flared at eye level. "We're waiting for a third person before we order." As soon as the waiter backed away, Clara renewed her attack, determined to get some reaction from Arthur. "Why, you lived for years with Larry, without ever telling me about him. The only time you ever mentioned him was two years ago when..."

"Three."

"Okay, three years ago, when you said, 'Larry's left me.' Until then I didn't know a thing about him, hadn't even heard his name, because until there'd been a few years of those silly antics out in the street, you never felt free enough, even with me, to..."

"Larry's dead."

"What?"

"I got a call last month from the hospital. He asked for me. He lasted another two weeks, almost. Conscious right up to the end. I was with him when he died." Two large tears had suddenly popped from Arthur's widened eyes, rolling down his cheeks into his beard. His eyes narrowed again, but he made no attempt to brush the tears away.

"Oh, Arthur, I'm so sorry. But he wasn't very old?"

"Forty-two."

"What...?"

"Kaposi's sarcoma," Arthur said, flatly, as he would pronounce a technical musical term he did not expect Clara to know. "Ever hear of it?" Clara shook her head as the waiter appeared with water, silverware, and napkins for three. They sat in silence until he was gone. "You will, I suspect. A rare form of cancer. It's showing up here, in New York, in L.A. A couple of new cases every week, the doctors told me, and almost all gay men. Young gay men. Larry was pretty old for Kaposi's. It is often combined with a rare form of pneumonia. Larry had that too, but it was the cancer that killed him. One or the other is usually fatal. And fast."

Arthur picked up his spoon, stirred his tea, then put the spoon down again. His look of irritability had completely disappeared, replaced by the grief it had masked. A slight wetness remained at the inner corners of his eyes. "The doctors think both diseases are associated with a breakdown in the body's immune system. Nearly all the victims have a history of repeated, multiple infections, and heavy drug use. Amyl nitrite, possibly. You know, poppers?"

Clara shook her head.

"Perfectly legal. Sold as a 'room odorizer.' When inhaled it's supposed to enhance orgasm. Larry and I had our first quarrel over my refusal to try it. I didn't tell you about that?"

"You never mentioned him until he left. I don't know anything about him."

Arthur kept his eyes directed downward. "I met him just after I moved to San Francisco. He was eight years younger than I, just turning thirty, but he looked much younger." Arthur raised his eyes to Clara's and gave a crooked smile. "He had a golden look about him." The smile vanished. "He moved in with me right away, and for a while things were fine. He'd been an art major at State, did a minor in speech therapy. That was how he earned his living, but he hated it. I was making enough. And he was so talented! I encouraged him to stay home and paint more. Maybe that was a mistake. When the work goes badly, you know, you have to somehow push past, keep pushing till you're loose and moving freely again. Larry had no patience for that. Pretty soon he wasn't doing much work at all. He began to accuse me of cramping his life. He said we were missing everything that would inspire him."

"Missing what?"

Arthur made a gesture with his hand, as if to include all that surrounded them. "The gay revolution. He said it was too late for me, but he could still pass for twenty-five." Arthur was silent while the waiter poured more tea, then backed away. "He started going out without me. The phone would ring at odd hours, men I didn't know. Then he began disappearing on weekends. He was gone for two weeks while I was moving into the big house. I tried to ignore it all. I was busy getting the school going. I thought he'd have a fling and get over it.

"We stopped having sex after I caught syphilis from him. He needed more and more money, for drugs, I suspect. The drugs began to affect his mind. Once, in the middle of an argument, he grabbed a knife—that wasn't like him. He was gentle—wild, but gentle.

"Then he came down with an intestinal disease, one of those parasites that used to be confined to tropical Africa. By the time it was diagnosed properly he was quite weak. I nursed him through it, then issued an ultimatum, not only for my sake. I didn't want him around the kids unless he gave up all that.''

Arthur's pause seemed unendurably long. "What did he say?'' Clara demanded.

Arthur shrugged, almost smiling at Clara. "He said, 'Don't be such an old-time queer.'''

"Oh, Arthur, I didn't mean. . . .'' Clara squirmed.

"And then he left. I never saw him again until the call from the hospital. He. . .his body was covered with herpes, and—no, I'll spare you the details. You see, he was utterly defenseless against infection. He was so full of morphine that half the time he didn't know me. The nurses said he had no other visitors, not one. All his lovers had disappeared, getting on with the gay revolution, I suppose.''

"Oh, Arthur, I don't know what to say.''

"Don't say anything. You helped me shed a tear for Larry. I haven't been able to, until just this moment. I haven't been able to talk about him. I have a room full of his paintings. I'd like to show them to you one day.''

Clara nodded. "It seems incredible. A man of such talent. How could anyone so well-endowed be so self-destructive? It's hard to believe.''

"Nonsense. You know better.'' Arthur's eyes were dry now, and his voice had regained its crisp, thrusting tone. "It's the rule, not the exception. Thoreau was right—all men's lives are failures. Oh, not yours. Maybe not mine. You do honest work. You serve life. But look at all the brilliant talents who've drunk themselves to death, or thrown away the work they were best at doing, or thrown away their energy on false crusades and called their means of self-destruction a sign of superiority. Larry did, almost to the end. Or how many take the opposite way out, like your parents, shut down and closed up, cringing to death? Why? Are they too afraid to live? Or too proud? Who knows? But it's the rule, not the exception. Larry's suicide was only more dramatic than most. Of all the seed, of all the fetuses, of all the infants, all the children, all the men and women... how few survive each stage and grow to the next, and how few of that few survive. Only a few, a tiny few beneficiaries of the right combination of genes and circumstances and decisions survive to begin to become human beings. And of those few—oh, Clara, interrupt me, don't let me go on ranting.''

Clara took his hand. "You need to grieve."

"Not now. Enough for now. Don't let me keep up this self-pitying, maundering—talk about something else. How's your love life? Are you going to marry that nice boy, what's his name? And is he old enough to vote yet?''

Clara laughed. "Walter's thirty-seven, and he has to go back to Maine at the end of the year. He's already started putting pressure on me to go with him. I try not to think about it. Or about what it was like before he came."

"Why not go with him?''

"And leave my work? My friends? What would I do in Maine? And don't tell me to make him stay here. His kids are in Maine. They need him, and he needs them.''

"What will you do when he leaves?''

Clara tried to laugh again. "Try to learn from my alcoholics —one day at a time. Maybe Walter and I will connect up again. Maybe not. I suppose there are worst things than living alone. And you? Hasn't there been anyone since Larry?''

Arthur looked bored. "A couple of men I have nothing in common with. Regular as conjugal visits to a prison. All quite apart from my friends, my work.'' He sighed, then smiled.

"Unlike you, however, I am more optimistic. Some day some other old-time queer will loom on the horizon, and I will not spend my final days alone. Well, have we talked enough about our sex lives to demonstrate our new freedom? I think so. And where in hell is Frank?"

"He got a late start to see the parade. He should be here soon."

"Well, I'm famished. Let's order and he can eat when he gets here. Where's our waiter?" Clara looked around, puzzled. She could not tell which of the swiftly moving young men had served their tea. Arthur motioned to one of them and ordered a cheese and fruit platter. "That, at least, will keep me from chewing on the table until he gets here. Well, how is he? How does he look?"

"I haven't seen him yet. He was going to come up to Ukiah for a weekend, but caught the flu, so today's the big reunion. You know, he did a wonderful piece for *Gay Streets*. I have a copy with me if . . ."

"I saw it."

"What did you think? Good, wasn't it?"

Arthur nodded summarily. "Sort of thing Frank can do with his left hand. Hartzler's a standard feature of gay media. If he didn't exist, they'd have to invent him. Perfect symbiosis. Are you cold?" He moved as if to offer his side of the table, which was sunnier, but Clara shook her head. Since the mention of Larry's death, she had felt a growing chill, yet the sun on her head felt uncomfortably hot.

"Why did Frank come back? I thought he was making a pretty good start up there."

Clara nodded. "He seemed to like it at first. Only complained that he was having trouble making ends meet."

"My teachers are underpaid too. My only defense is, so am I. His teaching load sounded heroic."

"Yes," said Clara, "but I thought he was perfect for the kind of place where you have to teach French and algebra and history, then conduct the chorus and coach the swimming team. For someone like Frank, who is so good at everything ...he didn't seem to mind that. He was lonely, of course."

"Of course, he would be at first."

"And his letters started complaining about the school being claustrophobic, ingrown, isolated."

"I thought he was near Vancouver."

"About an hour's drive."

"Well, he'll find any teaching job hard to come by here. The opening at JSB isn't for another two years, when Amy retires. I told him before he left—that I couldn't promise anything, but that when she retires he would be my first choice."

Clara shook her head. "He says he doesn't want to teach at all. He...hates it. Of course, he's right about the enormous amount of work for little pay. He's the one who must decide if the rewards are enough. You can't decide that unless you try it. You never really know until you're on your own in that classroom. It isn't as if he has to stay in work he doesn't like. He doesn't have anyone depending on him for...the only way to find out what is right...for him...is...." The chill had now settled into a cold, hard mass in her mid-section, freezing her breath. She had been forcing out the words, and now they too seemed to freeze under Arthur's direct, cool gaze. "What are you thinking, Arthur?"

He made a little lifting, flipping gesture with his teaspoon. "*Deja vù.* We seem to have this conversation every year or so, as Frank changes jobs or course of study, or drops out or in again. At first he was going to be a mathematical genius."

"That was only a childhood game. He never really studied; though, of course, he still knows more math than most high school math teachers."

"For a while I thought I was going to make a musician out of him. I never saw anyone pick up notation so fast," said Arthur. "But introducing him to Balinese scales sent him off into eastern civilization."

"His major at UCLA was psychology. You remember that field study he did on therapy for gays. But he didn't want to be a therapist, so he tried court reporting school when he came back here."

"Why did he quit that?" asked Arthur. "I thought he was supposed to make pots of money at it."

"As a glorified stenographer. He was bored to death. I was glad when he gave up that idea."

"Didn't he do creative writing at San Francisco State for a while?"

Clara nodded. "But you can't earn a living writing fiction."

"So now that he's dumped teaching, what's next?"

"That's up to him, isn't it!" Instantly Clara regretted her defensive tone. "I mean...you know...our generation had fewer choices than his. With more choices, you have more problems." She was beginning to feel Arthur's laser look again. "I've said that before too." He nodded, and Clara shrugged. "Okay. Okay."

She felt herself collapsing into confession, like a criminal who can hold out no longer, must let go, abandoning loyalty to an accomplice. "I have Frank's last letter with me. Don't ask me why I've been carrying it around for weeks."

As she pulled the letter out of her purse, she heard her name called. "Lontana. Clara Lontana?" The waiter was setting the food on their table as he looked around. "Anyone out here by that name? Phone call for Clara Lontana."

"That's me." Clara stood. The waiter pointed toward the doorway into the bar. "Probably Frank, still down on Market Street. I hope he hasn't met some friends and decided to stand us up." She handed the letter to Arthur. "Read this while I'm gone and tell me what you think."

March 24, 1980

Dear Mom,

I'm sorry I hung up on you. I'd have called back right away except that the expense doesn't seem justified when I would only repeat what I obviously haven't been able to make clear. I hope that by writing, I can put together the fragments of ideas and thoughts from our recent letters and phone calls, achieving some kind of clarity which will help you understand why I'm coming home.

You always told me you wanted me to feel free to make my own mistakes, to find my way as I must, that no one should tell me what I <u>had</u> to do, as you were told when you were young. Yet now you ask if a few months is long enough to decide I hate this place. You repeat that the first couple of years of teaching are the hardest. In other words, you cancel out those fine words about free choice by implying that I should stay in a situation I hate, until I get used to it. The way you stayed at Continuation for six miserable years, hating it from the first day? Or stayed in your marriage with Dad for over ten years, when you never really wanted to marry him? You always said you didn't want me to live by the rigid parental demands, or the depression-poor fear, or the limited choices of your generation. But your suggestion that I stay on here longer sounds like a reversion to the fear of independent experiment which you began to conquer only when you reached the age I am now. It also seems designed to subtly hint that I don't know my own mind.

Regarding this job and the people here, there is no question in my mind. They are narrow, smug, ingrown, elitist, incapable of letting a breath of air into their stuffy little farcical imitation of the senile headmaster's conception of what Eton was in 1910.

The incident I told you about, when he criticized the way I had deviated from the deadly drill they've followed in French for the past three generations, is only a symptom of the impossibility of injecting anything living into this place. I won't go into it again.

Yes, I know I've turned about face from the way I felt about this school in the beginning. And I did agree with you that teaching and influencing those who are likely to wield power some day is as worthwhile as teaching the poor, and more pleasant. I'm not denying that the kids here are bright and the other teachers are better educated and better read than most of the teachers I had in school. But I see how they're getting fossilized too.

I wrote you right after that meeting, so I won't describe all over again their reaction to my proposal for curriculum change. You said it was too soon, that I have to keep quiet for a year or two "while you size up the situation, then gradually take on responsibilities, proving you have sense and stamina, then gradually suggesting changes." No doubt you are right. No doubt, ten years of chipping away at the edges of this monolith would achieve some of the changes it needs. But I can't see giving years of my life for so small an accomplishment. I'd die of boredom before I managed it.

That brings me to your advice that even if I hate the place, it's important to be hired for the second year, so that when applying to another school later, it would be quite clear that nothing was wrong with my teaching. I'd agree with you—if I wanted to teach. There is now no question whatsoever in my mind that I never want to enter a classroom again.

Most of the kids, even in a selective school like this one, are only interested in picking up what they need in order to secure the jobs that will give them money and status. That's damned little in the case of the kids from the really rich families. And the ones who study hard are just grinds who, every time they raise their hands to ask a question, say, "Will that be on the test?" or come to talk to me only about raising the grade on a paper, not about really improving it.

I've got about three kids in each class, as I told you, who possess true intellectual curiosity, who haven't already shut down operations as thinking human beings. When you wrote that that was a pretty good number, better than average, you made up my mind for me. You've become so used to it, that you can say such a thing and not be shocked. I'm shocked. I can't see putting all my energy into an effort for such low returns. Or battering away at walled minds in the hope of opening a few more. It may be a noble effort, but it's mostly a wasted one.

I'd have realized this before—from being a T.A. and just from being a student myself—if it hadn't been for your influence. Because teaching is everything to you, you can swallow all these things, and always have. You were always a teacher, as far back as I can remember. Even when you hated a school or an administration (and some of those long-term subs you took in Berkeley weren't any better than Continuation), you remained devoted to teaching.

What happened was that I absorbed that attitude from you. No matter what I saw, no matter what I really felt, I continued to assume unconsciously that teaching is the only important work to do in the world. Deep down, I remained convinced that after I "freely" experimented with other things, I'd end up teaching, like you, because there wasn't any other important work to do.

Now, up here alone through a miserable, barren winter that isn't over yet (are the plum trees still in bloom down there?) I've had plenty of time to think about what I really want, what I really am. I am not a teacher.

And I want to return to my home.

Your suggestion that I go elsewhere, "see more of the world," is a peculiar one for a woman who was born in California and hardly ever left it, instead going deeper into its backwoods. I know, I know—it was a different time, especially for a woman, and you had more than a child to keep you from exploration. There were other inhibitions, of which some traces remain even today. In any case, staying near your birthplace was not entirely your choice.

Yet you have said that since World War II, the world has come to the Bay Area. All the friends you made while I was growing up came from somewhere else. Came to the center of important changes. All through the sixties in Berkeley, when you dragged me from one demonstration to another, you kept saying, "Remember this, remember it started here, this is history in the making." You were right. I was proud of you, and proud to be with you.

Then how could you imagine that I should prefer any place to my home, where so many important events have happened and are happening? And where, like you, I have many friends who've come from other parts of the country. Why endure this frozen pseudo-English prep school, or another like it in middle America, or some dirty overcrowded place on the East Coast? For experience, you say. But remember, you also said that life is being lived everywhere; all places and people are important and interesting. If you can say that in defense of this backwater or the one where you live and work, why can't it apply to San Francisco, my home, and, as everyone agrees, the most beautiful city in the world.

Finally I can only repeat, reiterate and reemphasize—until the words if not the meaning get through to you—my fundamental reason for leaving this place. I refuse to live and work in a place where I must deny my sexuality. You think that because the headmaster knows I'm gay, all my problems are solved, my acceptance assured. To ask, "In what way do you need to assert your sexuality at faculty meetings and swimming meets?" seems a good joke to you. "You're not swishy anyway, so it's not your manner. . ." and so on, until hanging up was the only response I was capable of. No response is possible to a straight person who cannot imagine how much the values, the ambience, the assumptions of heterosexuality fill the air like a gas that chokes and stifles a gay person. For you to say that my sexual opportunities can't be worse than those of a fifty-year-old woman in Ukiah only shows how incorrigibly straight you are. And frankly, it's pretty arrogant, like a white person telling a black, "I know how you feel," when there's no way she could know.

I don't mean to hurt you. All I am saying is that the most well-meaning, least prejudiced straight person has no idea of the weight of oppression, the smothering of the natural expression of the sexuality which is as much a part of me as my voice, my breath, my heartbeat—the suppression of which I am conscious at every moment. It is a suppression I refuse to endure. And I need not endure it, because I have a home to return to and a community to welcome me and to support my efforts to build a life among my own kind.

I've given the headmaster my resignation, effective at the end of the term. I'll be home by June.

Love,
Frank

As he was finishing the last page of the letter, Clara moved into Arthur's peripheral vision, sinking back into the chair opposite him.

"I see Frank hasn't changed. He still comes on like a filibustering southern senator when he's not sure of his ground. This reminds me of some of the blasts he used to send from UCLA after an overdose of Freud and Szasz, an indigestible mix. Did he..." Arthur raised his eyes to look at Clara, then stopped, astonished. She had turned a grayish, dead color, like concrete, her eyes fixed in a shocked unseeing stare. "What's wrong?"

"Hepatitis. Frank has hepatitis."

"Oh shit. Here." Arthur pushed the cup of cooling tea at her and watched as she lifted it and drank. Her color did not return, but her eyes focused on him as she put down the cup.

"They called him from the clinic with test results."

"How bad is he?"

"He's had no fever for three days, and they told him that might mean he's over the worst of a light case. But he can't be sure because sometimes it takes an unexpected turn after a couple of weeks and...oh, God, all I can think of is those four people who died last year. I read about it in the paper. Where was it? Oakland. A worker in a doughnut shop had it. Thirty-eight people caught it, and four died."

"You didn't tell him that."

"Of course not." It was amazing to Arthur how old Clara suddenly looked. She was a sturdy woman with a strong brow, nose, jaw. Now suddenly the lines framing her mouth had deepened, pulling her entire face downward. She needed only a black shawl over her head to complete the picture of hopeless grief depicted in photographs of wartime Italy.

"What did they tell him to do?"

"Stay in bed. Eat no fat or alcohol. Call if he gets worse." Clara took a deep breath and nodded rather sternly, as if to herself, to quell her own panic. "He's been sick for over a week already, so the real danger is probably past. That's what I told him. He's lying there with a mirror, watching himself turn yellow, terrified. So am I. I tried not to show it, but I didn't succeed too well. On the other hand, he brightened a little when he sensed how worried I was." The lines pulling Clara's mouth downward loosened, lifted a bit. "He always does when he tells me he's sick, and I worry. It's like sharing the load or...."

"Or like vicarious atonement, best left to Jesus Christ," Arthur snapped. "Come on, Clara, I cannot stand an obsessive parent."

She nodded. "God, it's the same as when he was two and fell out of the car."

Arthur shook his head. Twenty years ago their friendship had begun with Clara confessing her unnatural feelings as a mother. What she called her maternal indifference was, he had told her, a simple insistence on having work and thoughts of her own. She seemed unaware of how much she actually gave to her maternal role. When Frank left, she was free, wasn't she? A woman who no longer had a child, her attention unified and focused, like Arthur's. Now, this sudden flood of maternity surprised him, mystified him, and slightly repelled him. "Look, if they didn't hospitalize him, it must mean he's got a light case, and it's just a matter of a few weeks' rest. Sounds like what I had."

"You had hepatitis?"

"Larry's parting gift." Arthur would soften nothing, refusing to regret that he had mentioned Larry. He could give anything to a friend like Clara—love, money, loyalty—but never a lie or evasion in the name of kindness. "We've all had it. There's a serum being developed at Stanford to immunize against it. They're testing it now, advertising for young gay men in this area. They're having a hard time finding anyone who hasn't already had it."

Clara showed no sign of hearing him. She was staring blankly again.

"So look around you. Practically every man you see is a recovered case of hepatitis, all alive, now immune." He did not feel compelled to tell her about the incurable chronic carriers, nor the possibilities arising out of permanent liver damage. She actually did look around. He followed her eyes following the lithe young men pivoting around the tables with their trays and platters. Until last month, they had been a hardly noticed part of the scenery of restaurants and bars. But Larry's death had changed their aspect, given their smiles and gestures a desperate frailty which Arthur now found unbearable. He saw Clara staring at one, then another, as if seeing them for the first time. Her eyes remained expressionless, mystified. One of the waiters smiled at her inquiringly, then approached with coffee, which she allowed him to pour into her empty tea cup.

She was pulling at the short, graying strands of hair above her ear, watching Arthur. "You got over it all right? No after-effects?" She stared intently. Arthur felt he was being examined for every possible sign of health.

"I can't drink much. I get queasy even with a glass of wine. So my liver has been left a bit touchy, I suspect."

"Otherwise you're all right?" she insisted.

Arthur nodded. "What are you going to do?"

"Frank said to finish lunch, then call him so he could give me a list of things to bring."

"You should keep away. He's highly contagious."

"Arthur, I must see him."

"Then keep far away from him. Don't touch anything. Don't use anything—towels, glasses. Wash your hands a lot."

"I will."

"And as soon as you get home, go to your doctor and get a gamma globulin shot."

"Will that protect me?"

"I don't know. It's the medical equivalent of the sign against the evil eye. Do it anyway, just in case."

"I will."

"And finish your lunch."

"I will." But Clara did not touch her food. Arthur poured cream into her coffee. Clara's hand shook as she picked up her cup. She put it down again, then grasped it with both hands and raised it to her lips, sipping slowly, looking vacantly above Arthur's head. Her shoulders sagged, then trembled.

"Dammit, Clara, we're not going to cure Frank's hepatitis by sitting here and brooding over it." He cast about for something to shake her out of her shivers. "I'm far more interested in talking about his letter."

Clara nodded slowly and steadily in determined agreement. She seemed to be gathering all her strength to obey Arthur, to bring her mind into control over her panic. "Yes," she said, in a low, controlled, hoarse voice. "Yes," she repeated, more strongly, with a nod that was supposed to be more vigorous and decisive, but looked more like a twitch caused by the jerk of an invisible string attached to her head. "Perhaps you can help me to understand his letter, especially the part about —denying his sexuality?"

"That's just the current rhetoric here. Read the rest of that paper his interview is in. Right between Frank's interview and the purple pages (the inset of sex ads) there's a speech by a gay candidate for city office. Same phrases—no work in which he would have to deny his sexuality. It's like an ethnic candidate or a black promising not to forget his roots and his people. It's popular among some gays to think of themselves as an ethnic, cultural minority, with a separate language and all. But I'm surprised at Frank copying that dumb analogy to being black, as if blacks ever had such a nice thing as a closet to come out of—or to get back into when things got rough. I hope you pointed that out to him."

Clara shook her head. "This letter ended the discussion. I didn't want his homecoming to be full of rancor toward me. So I dropped it." She sipped her coffee. "He thought I was being flippant, but I really don't understand what he means about having to deny his sexuality. There are gay people all over the world, aren't there? Living lives like other people, lonely, with problematical relationships, like mine with Walter. What does he mean?"

Arthur shrugged. "How should I know? Frank's experience has been different than mine. Has it occurred to you that it has been different from the experience of ninety-nine percent of all people? Gay or straight? Look—he left home to go to UCLA in 1968, when there was already a fairly active gay culture in L.A. He came back here in 1972, when Castro Street was exploding into a gay settlement. From the age of eighteen, except for this past year in Canada, Frank has lived, grown to maturity, in a world of instant, casual, even anonymous sex. That's a world you and I and most people in the world, gay or straight, of any culture or era, can't even imagine, let alone describe.

"This year up there has been his first experience with what we know as normal relations among *all* the sexes. It must feel damned frustrating, even like persecution to someone who is a virgin, so to speak, when it comes to real sexual relations. That never occurred to you?"

"It seems to me..." All the strength of reason had come back to Clara's face. It was her beauty. "...that I did not let it occur to me. I refused to think about that, in regard to Frank." She spoke the words like a judgment on herself. For her it was a harsh judgment, so harsh that Arthur worried that she might sink again under its weight. "What you're describing," she said, "is the life Larry left you for."

Arthur shrugged. "Probably not to that extreme. How promiscuous is Frank, do you know? Does he cruise baths? Bars? Toilets?"

"Baths," Clara said. "Bars." She swallowed, and her chin trembled, but she looked squarely at Arthur. "Never toilets. We talked about that once, when one of my colleagues was arrested, lost his job. Frank was quite contemptuous, said toilets were for closet cases."

"That's not entirely true, but...anyway," Arthur pursued, "how often? Twice a week? Every night?" He took a breath, deciding to spare her nothing. "Larry once boasted he'd had twenty-three contacts in one weekend." Clara only looked blank. "But I'd guess Frank has too many other interests to throw himself away like that. What did he tell you?"

"Very little. He told me when he caught syphilis at the baths. I didn't know...so he started describing what the baths were. I...didn't really listen. I didn't want to know. As soon as I was sure he was getting treated, I...we...didn't talk any more about that."

86

"What are his friends like?"

"I don't know. I've never met any of them."

"Not one?"

Clara shook her head. "Couple of times when I was in town and called, he said he was busy. He preferred to spend a weekend in Ukiah occasionally. I got the feeling he didn't want me to visit him here, or to meet his friends."

"You never asked him why?"

Clara kept shaking her head. "I didn't want to interfere, force myself. I didn't want to be like my parents, prying, touchy and uptight, always condemning what they didn't understand."

"But, dammit, you're nothing like your parents. Now that Frank is grown up, you two should be friends."

"We are...I tried to...I thought that we...."

"Bullshit! You sound to me as if you behave toward Frank the same way you do toward your parents, walking on eggs, avoiding unsafe subjects, never speaking your mind. You don't seem to speak out honestly to him, anymore than to your parents. Yet you two are supposed to be close, supposed to share the same values."

"I guess I was trying to protect that closeness."

"By not saying what you thought?"

"I didn't want to start quarrels that would hurt our relationship, provoke letters like that one."

"Arguments are part of a close relationship. You argue with me."

"You're not my son."

Arthur sighed. "Let's talk about the rest of his letter. That I can understand. So can you. First year teaching grumbles. Everything he says is true. Inertia is killing. New teacher gets the crap. We all know that, and anyone who wants to teach just lives with it and resists as well as he can."

"If he wants to teach," said Clara. "Frank just doesn't want to teach."

Arthur raised his eyebrows. "I'm not so sure of that. I doubt Frank is, either." Arthur leaned back, studying Clara. Her color was good. She was thoughtful, shaken, but no longer in a state of shock. "Here's a shot in the dark, just a hunch. Has it occurred to you that Frank is afraid?"

"What could he be afraid of?"

"Of failing."

"Frank?" At last he had made Clara smile. "Frank can do anything."

"And has," Arthur said. "That's just it. The great danger for someone as talented as Frank is the immediate success as a beginner. Applause. It's addictive. You can become so addicted to the applause given for an impressive beginning that it overshadows interest in the work itself. When the applause stops, can the bright beginner settle down to work? I've lost some good students who were spoiled by early applause, praise, facility. They seemed to hold some underlying conviction that, really, they were fakes, and that if they kept up, they'd be found out. I still say his letter sounds scared, a temporary loss of nerve. He'll get started moving again."

"Frank's thirty," said Clara. "Almost. Late to be starting again."

"Clara, look at us, you and me. We were near forty before we touched firm ground."

"Yes," Clara agreed, "but at thirty we turned in the direction of the place we were heading for."

"Oh, I'm tired of talking about Frank. And I will not allow you to sink back into that quagmire of maternal goop! I want to tell you about the marathon concert the kids are doing at JSB, a benefit for Amnesty International. I've got this mezzo, a sixteen-year-old black girl like nothing you've ever heard."

Arthur left Clara in the phone booth in front of the bank. She watched him weave through the crowds, his head held straight, never turning to acknowledge the presence of the crowds, mostly men, who moved in bunches of five or six, swirling like waves around him, unable to avoid bumping against him, against each other, against the booths which stood in a line down the middle of Castro Street. The crowds continued to swell as more people flowed in from Market Street, spilling off Castro to side streets, then moving back up toward the center of the festivities again.

While she stood in the glass booth dialing Frank's number, Clara watched the groups of men, many of whom had shed their shirts to reveal well-muscled shoulders. Frank had often mentioned his faithful workouts at a gym, wherever he might be living. She had approved what she saw as his devotion to physical health. Now, looking at these men holding their taut shoulders erect, she realized they must all exercise with weights, and not for health but for beauty. They held themselves as women did, ever aware of their appearance to others.

Yet the longer she watched them, the more they reminded her of the Castro Street of the 1950's, those tense days when homosexuality was unmentionable, when women belonged in the home, when men all looked alike, relentlessly cropped, squared-off, "masculine." If anything, these men in the street now looked even more uniform and stiff, not like the real men of the fifties but like the hard, slim mannequins in the store windows of those days.

A crowd of them waited to get into a bar. A golden-haired boy in uniform admitted them two or three at a time as the same number left the brimming-over, glass-walled corner. Inside, men sat in bright light behind the glass windows, facing outward, like merchandise on display. These places were completely different from the solid-walled, dark bars of older times, where people drank as if in shame. Yet darkness was not abolished. Who had hinted to her of the existence of a dimly-lit back room for quick sexual consummation of connections made near the brightly lit windows? Probably Frank, at some time or other, but she had chosen not to hear him until now.

Clara turned away from the thought, literally turned her back on the scene and saw, staring at her through the glass of the phone booth—a woman, painted blood-red and chalk white under brass hair, with breasts like huge funnels raising peaks in her red sequined gown. No, of course, not a woman, a man in grotesque parody of a 1940's movie queen, making a savage grin at her before he waved and danced outward toward the center of the street. When he raised his arms, she noticed that his arm pits were shaved, and their unpainted skin was black.

The phone had been ringing and ringing. She fastened her eyes on it, as if to ask it why Frank was so long in answering. Sudden panic weaved a scenario: his fever had risen again and he was too weak to answer; he was delirious; in his delirium he had heard the phone and risen from bed; he had fallen, hitting his head; he was unconscious, injured, bleeding to. . . .

"Hello-o." Frank's voice cracked into a breathy giggle at the end of his answer. There was noise in the background: voices, laughter, music, then Frank saying, "Cut that," and the music dying down. "Hello." Now his voice was peremptory, demanding, almost strong, with little of the stark, shivering panic with which he had announced the test results an hour ago.

"You sound better."

"What? Mom? I can't hear you."

"You have visitors?"

"Yeah. After I talked to you, Benjy showed up with some guys he picked up at the parade. Do you know how to cook halibut? This crazy Benjy went across the street and came back with this big stinking fish, low-fat protein, proper diet for hepatitis."

"You could bake it."

"What temperature? How long?" His next words were lost in a general roar of laughter, which Frank joined in a breathy chuckle. When it subsided, he said, "Look, when you come by later, maybe you could cook it. And bring some canned soup too, not the cream type, and fruit, lots of fruit. That's supposed to be good for me."

"Aren't your visitors afraid of catching. . . ."

"Oh, they've all had it. They're immune. You know, plague of the gay community."

"Then let them cook your fish for you." Clara immediately regretted the edge of anger in her voice. In time of trouble, of fear, of need, she mustn't fall into anger as her parents had. Frank's friends had cheered him up, eased the fear that, in her own panic, she could only share, perhaps even increase. They evoked his bravery, or bravado. Whatever it was, it made him laugh, and that was good for any illness.

"Oh, they're on their way out to the show at the Castro Theater." The noise around him and around her glass cage had drowned out her angry tone, or he simply had not noticed. "Hey, be quiet, will you, I'm trying to hear. . . yeah. . . you better, if you're going to get there in time. Sure. Have a good time. Right. Bye." Clara heard doors close, then silence. "They're gone, I can hear you now."

"I'm glad they cheered you up."

"Well, I guess they're right. Like they said, it was just my turn. Colin was going to make me a little certificate and do an initiation rite over the fish, but that kind of cheering up gets a little macabre for me. Besides, I'm tired. This thing really wrings me out. I'm lucky I got such a light touch of it. Rex was in the hospital for two weeks. I was never that sick."

"You shouldn't overdo, Frank, even if you feel better."

"Oh, sure. I'm going to stay right in bed. Theo brought me this video tape rig to attach to my television. It costs about a thousand, but he works at this TV place and can get me a discount if I want to keep it. And Benjy brought over his collection of Judy Garland tapes. He's got everything, even old TV specials most people have never seen. You ought to have one of these things. If you aren't home to watch a program, you can set it to tape automatically, and then you can watch it later."

92

"You used to say there was nothing on TV worth watching, let alone..."

"What? I can't hear you."

"I guess you're too sick to read. No point in bringing you any books?"

"No, I can't concentrate. I just lie here and meditate on the cracks in the ceiling."

"Yes." Clara swallowed and chose her words carefully. "I always see an illness as a time to stop and think..."

"Right."

"...because our state of health reflects our lives. An illness forces us to evaluate...to consider..." She hesitated, unable to be sure which would be the right words to suggest, not to offend, not to step into an emotional mine field and cause an explosion, especially while he was sick.

"Well, you don't want me to become a monk!" he laughed.

So she had not needed to find the words. He knew what she meant, knew and freely acknowledged how he had become sick, with no more reticence than the times he had called her as soon as tests confirmed syphilis. Was it twice, three times? The memory, so deeply buried, came back dimly: his nervously casual announcements, her silent prayer of gratitude for antibiotics. Was it after the time he learned he had been a symptomless carrier for months that she acquired the habit of changing, not only sheets, but towels, anything he had touched during a weekend visit to Ukiah?

"You still there?"

"Yes, Frank, I'm here."

"The background noise is awful. You must be right in the middle of everything."

"I'm on Castro and Eighteenth."

"Yeah. Well, up this end of Castro it's pretty quiet. Too steep a hill. Thank God I can get some sleep. What time is it?"

"Almost three."

"Look, I think I really just want to sleep as long as I can. I'm going to unplug the phone. You can take your time coming. Enjoy the street fair. Shop. You might even take in the show at the Castro. *Over The Rainbow.* After a lot of political stuff. In a good cause. I'll leave the front door unlocked and you can just come in when you get here. No rush. I just ate some fruit; I won't be hungry. All I want is sleep."

"All right, Frank. I'm sure that's best. I'll see you later. Soup and fruit. Anything else?"

"No. See you."

She waited for his click before hanging up. She felt in no hurry to leave the phone booth. It protected her from the crowds surging around her. There were more older people like her wandering about, looking at the booths, and some young couples with children. But the sounds she heard came from the groups of men who laughed in low rumbles or thin screeches as they rushed past, huddled, then rushed on.

Across the street a neat blue van was parked. The door was marked CITY HEALTH CLINIC. On the side of the van, in gold lettering, was the message

IF YOU DON'T WANT TO TALK ABOUT VD
LISTEN
495-O G O D   for taped information
on symptoms and cures

Clara put in a dime and punched 495 O GOD. Nothing happened. She had punched the wrong O, the zero instead of the letter O. Her dime jangled back to her. She put it through the slot again and punched the square buttons once more. A busy signal. She laughed as the steady, insistent, harsh beep sounded, punctuating her almost silent giggles. She was not sure which was more funny, that the VD line was busy or that, when she dialed GOD, she got only a busy signal. She waited for her giggles, like gut-wrenching hiccups, to subside before she opened the door and stepped out of the phone booth.

94

"Popsicles!" No, that wasn't it. "Cocksickles! Cocksickles! Get 'em while they're hard!" A young woman, very plump, wearing a stained purple shirt over large, tight jeans, waved a purple, penis-shaped ice on a stick. She drew another out of a steaming ice chest, extended both arms, waving them as if she held semaphore flags. "Cocksickles!" A few people smiled as they passed, but business seemed slow.

Clara let herself be pushed by the surging crowds toward the booths standing in a close line down the middle of the street. Tapestry, paintings, bowls, earrings, books—the same art and craft booths as at any street fair. There were some differences, like the table which held only lists of mail order products. Chief among them was an oil vaguely described in strings of adjectives: sensuous, fulfilling, silken. Another list was headed ENHANCERS. A man leaned over the table to discuss the lists with men who stopped, but he ignored Clara.

Clara made slow progress through closely packed bodies in groups which seemed content with little movement, except to shout a greeting to someone or to applaud a dancing drag queen. Finally she was able to cross the sidewalk and duck into a more quiet, almost dark shop.

A line of glass unicorns with sharply pointed, long horns stood on black velvet stands, lit artistically from below. Clara leaned against a greeting card rack. IS SEX DIRTY? asked one of the cards, in heavy black letters. She picked it up and opened it for the answer: YES, IF YOU DO IT RIGHT. The rest of the store contained ceramic wall plaques, picture frames, glass bowls, bells, noseless busts of Alexander, and more glass unicorns on black velvet. She looked at the address. If memory served, this had been the campaign headquarters of Harvey Milk.

She moved out onto the street again, hugging the walls of shops where she felt less likely to be caught up and pushed along with moving groups. She passed another store; more ceramic ornaments, cheaper gadgets, badges, greeting cards. This one was brightly lit with flashing colored lights. It reminded Clara of those shops that had sprouted on Mission Street during the war, leeching money from homesick sailors. She passed a men's clothing store, ALL AMERICAN BOY. One display window held colored T-shirts and jeans. The other was stacked to the top with brown teddy bears.

". . . purveyors of filth, you can sell dirty books while your soul rots, but there's only one book and that's the *Bible* and it takes only one word from that one book, the word of God, that's all you need, not this propaganda of Sodom with the devil's badge engraved on your heart and . . ."

That voice again. Clara peered across the street, looking for the green coat, locating the mad, ranting woman near the blue van. She began to make her way into the street again to see who the old woman was yelling at this time.

She almost collided with a small man in tight leather pants. From the waist up, he was bare, brown and bony, except for loose flesh near his navel. His head was shaven on the sides but appeared to be naturally bald on top. The delicate chain earring hanging from one earlobe matched, in minature, the thick, metal chains looped around the black leather belt at his waist. On one side of the belt hung a coiled whip; on the other side, steel manacles jangled.

Clara was close enough now to see that the old woman was standing over a card table near the van, shaking her fist at the neat rows of pamphlets. No one paid any attention to her, but as she moved away from the table into the middle of the street, a line of six men passed between her and Clara. They were holding hands and skipping around in a ring. Other men broke into the chain, enlarging it until it encircled the old lady. She ignored or did not notice the dancing ring of men spinning around her. Clara watched, reminded of the chain of paper dolls she used to cut from long, folded strips of paper, then open out into a string of identical figures, holding hands. The circle opened as suddenly as it had formed, swerving into snap-the-whip, the man on the end screeching as he was flung wide, slamming into the side of the van, shaking, nearly upsetting the table which stood next to it.

Above the table streamed a banner which read GAY HEALTH. Tacked to the windshield of the van was a sign
FREE VD TEST HERE.
The side door of the van was open, but the inside was too dark to see anything. Two men leaned against the van. They wore straw hats, and on the front of their T-shirts large badges read   S.F.HEALTH DEPT.
MEN'S CLINIC
On the table were spread brightly colored pamphlets, cards, and two long sheets headed HEPATITIS SCREENING PROJECT.

"I say we're wasting our time, might as well pack up and go."

The second man nodded, pulling off his badge. "Mike was right. It doesn't pay to stay past two on any street fair day. The mood changes."

"I can take old Myrtle's raving, but if one more doped-out idiot propositions me to get into the van and make it with him. . . ."

"Spoilsport." He laughed as he pulled down the banner, tossing it into the van. "Anyway, I want to get a good seat at the benefit show. Let's close it up."

As the two men began to gather up papers from the table, Clara reached out and took a pamphlet.

Do You Love Your Fellow Man?

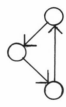

Then Protect Him and Yourself From

STDs

(sexually transmitted diseases)

DISEASE	SYMPTOMS	CURE
SYPHILIS	Painless sore at location of contact (penis, anus, mouth) Rash	Antibiotics
GONORRHEA	Burning, itching while urinating Discharge from penis No symptoms if in anus or throat	Antibiotics
NGU (non-gonococcal urethritis)	Burning, itching while urinating Discharge from penis	Antibiotics
NGP (non-gonococcal proctitis)	No symptoms	Antibiotics
HERPES	Painful sores on sex organs or in rectum Fever Abdominal pain Flu-like aches and pains	No cure Sores subside, break out in later attacks Highly contagious during outbreak of sores
OTHER INFECTIOUS SORES venereal warts granuloma inguinale lympho-granuloma venereum molluscum contagiosum chancroid	Sore on penis, anus, rectum	Chancroid cured by antibiotics Others subside without treatment, but often recur. Various lengthy treatments sometimes help.

Disease	Symptoms	Treatment/Outcome
SKIN AND HAIR PARASITES pediculosis crabs scabies	Itch Visible bugs in hair	Drugstore salves and powders cure crabs and pediculosis. Salve for scabies requires doctor's prescription.
"GAY BOWEL SYNDROME" amebiasis giardiasis shigella campylobacter	Severe abdominal cramps Constipation followed by diarrhea Gas Fever Bloating Weakness	Long course of treatment, often a year or more, with varying results; correct diagnosis by an experienced doctor is crucial. As these diseases become better known in the U.S. (usually found in undeveloped countries) diagnosis and treatment may improve.
HEPATITIS	Variable degrees of fever Nausea Weakness Flu-like aches Jaundice	No cure Most victims recover after a few weeks and are immune to future infection. A few remain chronically ill. Some remain symptomless carriers. Severe cases require hospitalization and may be fatal.
RECTAL INJURIES* anal fissures proctitis peritonitis	Pain Bleeding Fever	Usually major surgery followed by antibiotics.

*technically not disease but trauma-related results of inserting sexual toys, fists, and other objects

Protect Yourself Against Sexually Transmitted Diseases!

Many of these diseases have been redefined as sexually transmitted (as well as through contaminated water or food) by gay men, mainly through swallowing of urine, fecal material (shit), semen (cum), or other bodily fluids.

Unless you practice non-traumatic sex, involving minimal drug use, with one, exclusive lover, you are at high and rapidly increasing risk of contracting STDs.

If your lifestyle includes multiple sex contacts, you may reduce your chances of infection or injury by taking these precautions:

1. Use a condom, still the most effective protection against disease. If you are the passive partner, provide a condom for your active partner(s). Buy the best quality; cheap condoms are more likely to break during anal sex than during vaginal sex.

8. Do not use saliva as a lubricant. It carries and spreads germs.

9. Do not insert antibiotic creams or soap. These are of no proven use and may be dangerous.

10. Don't mix drugs and sex. Amyl nitrite (poppers) and other drugs are said to enhance sensation. But all drugs (including alcohol) affect judgment and deaden sensitivity to pain—your body's most urgent warning. In a group situation, especially with strangers, you may be at high risk for traumatic injury.

11. Never rim a stranger. The only interest of the health workers compiling this pamphlet is your well-being, not your lifestyle. But we must inform you that if you do oral-anal (ass-licking) sex outside an exclusive, monogamous relationship, in San Francisco, you will surely contract gastrointestinal disease and hepatitis.

In group situations where participants alternate penile-anal (fucking) sex with penile-oral (sucking) sex, the risk is also very high.

12. Have routine tests for STDs at least once a month. Many bath houses provide on-site testing for syphilis and gonorrhea. The VD van will be in your neighborhood at least once a week. All health centers provide free testing for all types of STDs.

13. If you develop obvious symptoms (sore, rash, burning sensation while urinating) you can get immediate treatment by going directly to the VD Clinic at 250 Fourth Street. Don't delay!

14. Immediately inform all sexual contacts if you have contracted an infection. Give names and phone numbers to the VD Clinic. This information is strictly confidential and essential to fighting disease. Anonymity is the greatest health hazard of the gay community.

15. Tell your doctor you are gay. Give him complete details of your sex practices so that he will know, for instance, whether to culture your anus or throat for gonorrhea. If your present doctor is unsympathetic to your lifestyle, contact the Gay Switchboard for a list of informed, non-judgmental doctors.

2. Exchange names and phone numbers with your partner(s). If he refuses, insist on giving him your phone number. Then there is at least a chance that he will call to inform you if you have become a symptomless carrier.

3. Wash with soap and water before and after sex. Taking a shower together should become a ritual in your lovemaking.

4. Make love with the lights on, examining your partner for sores, rashes, or other signs of infection. You can do this in the shower or as part of foreplay. If your partner mentions that he is just getting over a cold or flu, think twice.

5. Urinate immediately after sex, then wash with soap and water.

6. Do not use rectal douches. They may spread infectious bodies and/or alter the naturally protective balance of mucous membrane secretions.

7. Avoid scented lubricants; they cause irritation of anal membranes.

16. Follow your doctor's complete course of treatment exactly and thoroughly. Do not stop taking medication when symptoms disappear. Infection may upsurge again without symptoms, continuing to damage your health while making you a carrier of the disease to others. New strains of syphilis and gonorrhea are proving resistant to antibiotics and may require long treatment under your doctor's supervision.

   Do not take an old, left-over antibiotic for a new infection. It may have lost effectiveness, or may not be the right one for this new infection. Do not take your friend's or roommate's medication. It may not be the right one for your problem.

17. Remain under doctor's care even if (as in the case of herpes, venereal warts, or hepatitis) there is no medically certified cure. Counseling is available for patients with chronic hepatitis or herpes. You owe it to yourself and to the gay community to get help in dealing with the fact that you are a carrier of serious disease. Remember, the counseling service is the first to know about new treatments.

18. Join the hepatitis project. Over seventy percent of gay men in San Francisco have had hepatitis and are now immune. At least ten percent more are chronic, often symptomless carriers of hepatitis.

    You can help fight this terrible disease. Successful creation of a serum to immunize against hepatitis is near completion. This serum is made from the blood of hepatitis carriers.

    SIGN UP NOW for our free testing program. If you are a recovered hepatitis patient, free of the disease, you will be happy to learn that good news. If you have never had hepatitis, you may sign up for serum innoculation and gain protection as soon as it is available. If you know, or learn through testing, that you are a carrier, you will receive free counseling and may earn up to $100 per week providing blood for serum production.

Over the row of glass and wrought-metal doors of the Castro Theater a white banner stretched, its gold letters reading HARVEY MILK POLITICAL FUND.

Stationed at each door were the men in black nuns' habits. One of them wore a wimple which extended upward from his head in two parts, like stuffed rabbit ears or horns or phalluses. He smiled as he took Clara's five dollars, showing red lipstick smeared over his front teeth. He handed her a small card, like the "holy" cards portraying the Virgin Mary earned by Clara's childhood friends for memorizing their catechism, forced on Clara by the nuns who had pursued her. This card depicted a benign, dignified, bearded nun above a telephone number.

A short, stocky, older man, bearded like the picture on the card and dressed in a fuller, more carefully pleated black habit, stood just inside. Someone called, "Mother, mother!" and he hurried toward one of the "sisters" standing at the doors.

Clara walked past the candy counter in the narrow foyer and through the open doorway on the right. She sank into an aisle seat in the back row of the nearly empty auditorium and closed her eyes, which burned under the lids. Her legs ached as if she had walked miles. She tried to make her mind blank.

Unlike most old movie houses that survived at all, the Castro had not been cut into small compartments nor stripped and redecorated. After a period of dilapidation, it was carefully restored. The rosy murals on the walls suggested dusky sunsets in a classic Italian garden. The walls rose to a dome, its plaster painted to resemble copper, with gold-framed paintings set into the high arches. Clara opened her eyes to see exactly what she had seen there forty years ago, even to the small organ in front of the broad stage and the shimmering velvet curtain behind it. Her mind slipped back to a precise hour of a precise day, December 7, 1941.

For some reason she had not gone to the El Capitan on Mission Street, where noisy boys and girls from both sides of Mission Street converged on Sunday afternoons. It could not have been the picture that brought her to the Castro. No one cared what the picture was. They came to talk, laugh, walk about, munch candy and watch the older boys and girls smoking and necking. Why at the Castro on that Sunday? Oh, yes, it was the birthday party of Eleanor, a schoolmate who lived near Castro Street. Her parents had stuffed the six girls with cake and ice cream, then dropped them at the Castro Theater.

Clara could not remember when the quiet had begun to spread over them. Suddenly she noticed that even the boys were sitting quietly in their seats, not talking, not even eating, staring at the screen, but not as if they cared what was on it. One by one, children got up and walked out into the lobby, then silently returned to their seats, not looking at their friends, eyes fixed on the screen.

Finally, it was Clara's turn. As if summoned, she got up and walked the slightly inclining aisle, which seemed suddenly very steep, toward the lobby. She felt as if everyone were watching her, knowing what she did not know, where she was going and why, though no one turned away from the screen to glance at her.

Out in the lobby, ushers stood in solemn groups, not caring what rules were being broken inside, their admonitory flashlights dark and dead in their hands. They spoke in whispers. A radio sat on the glass candy case, and the manager stood over it, listening intently. A few children stood, like Clara, unnoticed, silent, ignored. Clara could not remember exactly who told her Japanese planes had attacked Pearl Harbor or what Pearl Harbor was. She could never remember actually hearing the word *war* mentioned by anyone. But somehow, like the other children, she took in the information. Then she turned, entered the auditorium and found her way through the darkness back to her seat.

None of the children left before the end of the movie. None of the girls she had come with spoke to each other as they sat there. Twice Clara heard someone crying, over to the left, then far down in front. The crying was quickly hushed. It was unseemly, pointless, self-dramatizing, too puny and self-indulgent a response to whatever awesome thing they all felt beginning. Clara always remembered that afternoon as the one moment in World War II when everyone around her acted in a manner appropriate to the reality of the war—those confused children, ignorantly solemn for an hour before they straggled home.

Suddenly the theater was full, and almost as noisy as it had been before the silence fell on that Sunday afternoon so long ago. People sat talking or stood waving and calling to friends across the theater. Some rushed up and down the aisles, or wandered slowly looking for friends or for empty seats. There were twice as many men as women. The largest group of women sat in the rear, on the other side of the theater from Clara.

A man and woman came out onto the stage together. A short rattle of applause came from scattered groups in the auditorium but was drowned out by the continued talking, laughing, and shouting. The woman smiled, raised her arm, and spoke, but her words were lost in the noise. The man handed her a microphone and her voice came over loud, but none too clear. "We. . .to welcome you all on another Gay Freedom Day. . ." Loud cheers rose, then fell to a steady buzz of talk. "Out. . .in the street, we've all had fun, but you are the ones who put your money where your mouth is . . .important political and social programs for gay people, for all people. Recipients from this benefit show include the Gay Switchboard, the Gay Anti-Nuclear. . . ." Her voice became just another sound in the increasing noise. There were hisses and shouts of "Quiet!" but they only added to the din. The woman read her list to the end, then looked around and shrugged.

The man took the microphone from her. "Hey, now, let's have some quiet so we can get started!" His voice boomed out over the noise, which subsided, then rose again as something happened in a far corner near the stage. Clara could not see what it was; she only heard the now familiar falsetto screeches, rippling off to low rumbling laughter across the heads turned in that direction. The man's next announcement was unclear, but was greeted by a mild cheer. Four people, two men and two women, stepped to the microphone. They began to sing in pleasant harmony, and gradually the audience quieted so that Clara could hear some of their lyrics.

They began with political lyrics attached to old folk songs, like the songs Clara had learned in demonstrations for civil rights and peace. One song warned gays to "walk in threes" alert to possible attack on the street. Another—sung to the melody of "Swing Low, Sweet Chariot"—warned that Dan White's parole would one day be "coming for to carry him home."

Then they sang a song which attacked churches, and another, and another. The anti-religion songs seemed to make up the bulk of their repertory. The lyrics were set to what must be old traditional hymn tunes. Clara recognized the form, but not the hymns themselves. They must be Protestant, and they must be very familiar to most of the audience. Only that could account for the raucous laughter and cheering that broke out during the uninspired verses ridiculing middle-American Christianity. In a brief change of pace, they sang one song which liltingly satirized lesbians. Clara heard only a few words of it, ". . . ve-ry po-li-ti-cal . . . live on Va-len-ci-a . . . strict-ly mo-nog-a-mous. . . ." The rest was drowned out by raucous male laughter. Their final song went back to the religious theme. After a short conference, they announced it as "guaranteed to shake up 120 million Americans." It was something about Jesus performing oral sex. Through the cheers that drowned out the song, Clara heard little but the refrain repeated at the end of each verse, ". . . Jesus satisfies."

The quartet left the stage, and again the man stepped to the microphone, ". . . to tell you about the great program we have for you. Harry Britt and Sally Gearhardt are here to outline plans for political mobilization against the right." Cheers. "The Lesbian Chorus is going to sing." He gestured toward the large group of women in the rear. "We have scenes from a new play by the Oscar Wilde Players, and. . ." Sensing that he was losing the audience again, he cut short his announcement. ". . . much more. Now, comedian Arnold Scott."

Arnold Scott? The name was teasingly familiar, but buried too deep in memory for instant retrieval. Arnold Scott? Evidently this audience knew him well. As the houselights dimmed and a round circle of light was projected on the rose-red curtain, the cheers rose to a roar that almost drowned out the organ thumping a bouncy vamp of "The Man I Love." Arnold Scott?

Into the circle of light stepped a sparkling figure: gold nylon scoops of hair, body swathed in scales of shimmering gold like the tight, thin skin of a fish, from neck to floor. In one motion the spangled arms fluttered upward to wave to the audience, while one long leg stepped through a slit in the gold dress, showing the inevitable black net stocking, starred with more gold sequins. The man beside Clara howled. In front of her, men were drumming their feet on the floor and yelling into the thunder they made.

Arnold Scott, still around? He had been a star back in the fifties, when North Beach was still full of Italian restaurants, bars where patrons and waiters sang operatic arias, jazz clubs —and one or two places for tourists which featured a mild strip or female impersonators like Arnold Scott.

The definitive break between her and Dino—though the marriage lasted several more years—came with Arnold Scott. Dino insisted that taking the man from the Bakersfield office to the club where Scott was appearing would secure his promotion. Why not a good play or the Hungry I? No, this was a simple guy, Dino insisted, who'd asked specifically about shows like the one Arnold Scott was in. Then *you* go, she tried. No, they always wanted to get a good look at the wife when considering a promotion. This would clinch it; she couldn't deny him such a little thing.

It was not the money—fully a week's pay plus babysitter. It was her inability to make Dino understand why female impersonation offended her. The crude, stammering statement she tried to build had since become an axiom of feminist thought, refined to indisputable clarity. But twenty-five years ago, it was as if she spoke in tongues to a tolerant, bemused atheist.

Once at the night club, Clara decided she had been too stiff-necked. Arnold Scott did his Bette Davis and Tallulah Bankhead and Katharine Hepburn rather nicely. Clara drowned three drinks quickly, gulping toward a numbness she hoped would make a noisy evening with boring people pass quickly.

Then Scott sang, his voice husky and throaty, a convincing torch singer moaning for the faithless man he/she loved so desperately. It was clear that Arnold Scott performed this part of his act seriously and with great pride. He had invented a "woman" as close as possible to the current desires of men, and, what was more, had made her pathetically hurt, damaged, betrayed by "The Man I Love," who deserted, leaving "Stormy Weather." By the time he began "They're writing songs of love, but not for me. . . ." an enchanted silence had fallen over the audience, almost a sad, stricken silence, as if Scott had conveyed to the audience some hint of the true cruelty, the abyss of confusion and suffering that underlay the fact that such an audience could be in such a place watching such a performance.

The strain was too much for the man from Bakersfield. He leaned over Clara, making a loud, inane remark, then snapped his fingers for a waiter, signaling another round of drinks. Clara saw Scott flash a look toward him as he finished the song and bowed to sustained applause.

Then it was time for the comic part of the act. Scott began with a few generally smutty jokes, as he edged closer to the table where Dino's party sat. Gradually his jokes began to be aimed at the man from Bakersfield. Dino looked uneasy, but Clara giggled as Scott ripped out a falsie and threw it at the man. Then Scott became like a man-woman possessed, spewing out rapid-fire quips, attacking the man's potency, manhood, looks, intelligence, all with the voice and gestures of a screaming bitch. Suddenly he had become another sort of woman invented by men, pursuing relentlessly even when the laughter of the audience began to soften with uncertainty.

Clara's laughter did not. She guffawed. She swallowed the drink ordered during Scott's song, then fell again into helpless giggles. She had not laughed so much, it seemed, in years.

In the midst of a joke, the band started playing, probably signaled by the uneasy-looking manager who stood near the bar. Clara felt herself being pulled to her feet and led out of the nightclub as Arnold Scott sang, "I'll be seeing you in all the old familiar places. . . ."

The promotion never came through, and Clara knew that Dino silently blamed her. In a way it really was partly her fault. She never denied that, nor ever regretted it. She never saw Arnold Scott again, and, after a few years, never heard of him; that era of North Beach clubs was over. He was obsolete.

But he had evidently found a new audience, a young one at that. Clara thought he must be near sixty. How fine for him to have another go. She had always held a small soft spot for Arnold Scott, on the edge of her firm, feminist analysis of female impersonation.

He still did Bette Davis very well, if somewhat more broadly. He had added a fearsome Joan Crawford, brandishing a coat hanger. The end of each imitation was followed by howling, stomping applause. When he began to sing, Clara noticed a clear difference from his former style. Though dressed as a "woman," he dropped any female identity. He sang in a clearly masculine voice, and his gestures were those of a male queen, not of a performer who tries to create the illusion of being a woman. His tone was full of longing, as before, but longing of a man for a man—or of longing for something.

Though enthusiastic, this audience was not truly much more attentive than the man from Bakersfield had been. At the end of his song, he held up his hands to quiet the applause which had drowned out its ending. "Okay, boys, okay." He cracked a joke Clara did not hear, but which raised howls of laughter from the men in front.

He began strutting back and forth on the stage, pointing his finger out into the audience, questioning, "Why do women wear veils in Iran? Because they're so ugly!" Laughter drowned out part of the next question. "...with Liz Taylor? Well, have you ever counted up those chins? You'd need a calculator, honey." He moved and talked faster and faster, incited by this audience, as he had been by the man from Bakersfield, driving them to shouts and claps as he had driven the other to silence.

He quickened his pace, bringing the explosions of laughter closer and closer together, stepping on laughs with gestures and wiggles that brought new convulsions to be interrupted, like a fit of coughing and sneezing, by new laughs. It was as if he held almost the whole audience, tickling them toward the edge of hysteria, himself almost hysterical with his power. Soon he was merely calling out a name, making a half-heard comment and a rude gesture, while the laughter merged into a continuous roar.

He held up one hand to quiet the roar, then began a monologue that was immediately blurred by waves of laughter. It was something about a long drive. Clara heard very little. She was distracted by movement from the other side of the auditorium where the large group of women sat. Groans, rustling movements, then long hisses surrounded the few phrases from the stage which reached her. "...old hag with...over the spics in that cadillac with...oh, come on, girls, where's your sense of humor?" Scott was standing with hands on hips, looking toward the rear section, where the Lesbian Chorus sat, and where the hissing had begun.

Some of the women shouted in unison, "Sexist humor! Sexist!" Some were standing. One woman pointed at Scott and yelled, "Racist!" A loud male roar drowned her out.

Scott stood absolutely still. He waited until shouts and counter-shouts, clapping and laughing died almost to silence. Then he said, "You know, that's why they put cocks on weathervanes; a stupid cunt flapping up there would give erroneous reports."

The roar rose like thunder. The women were all on their feet, standing in a surging sea of yelling, whistling, stamping men. Clara stood too, but did not move. For a moment she watched the dark ecstasy of yelling, stomping and clapping which rose higher as the women marched out.

Clara turned toward the rear door, grateful to be near it. As she pushed it open, she saw a few men get up and move toward her. Fear rippled through her before she realized that they too were leaving in protest, in support of the women. As they hurried past her, she recognized two of them, the men from the VD van. They crossed the lobby to join the crowd of women standing near the candy counter.

Clara could think only of getting out into fresh air. As she reached the front doors, she heard Arnold Scott beginning to sing, "More than you know, more than you know...."

Clara emerged from the theater into a dense fog which had brought the long summer day to sudden, early dusk. She turned and began to walk up Castro Street, hardly seeing what was left of the crowds of people—now reduced to restless moving male groups in their uniform denim or sequins or leather. They brushed or bumped her as they passed; she was invisible to them too. Their shouts, laughter, spurts of music from contending radios diminished as she walked south, though the sharp rattle of bongo drums still created centers for circles of silently undulating dancers whose movements alternated between rhythmic jerks and reeling staggers. As she crossed Nineteenth Street, one dancer stumbled and fell across her path. She looked down to see a wide, vacant smile on his pale, wrinkled face. His hair was sprinkled with gray, like hers, but from the neck down, in tight denim, he was slim and taut, like a boy. She hardly broke her stride as she stepped over his body, men rushing behind her to pick him up as a policeman watched benignly from the opposite corner.

She welcomed the uphill climb, which few of the dancers were making. She walked faster, making her heart and lungs pump harder, faster. She counted her steps, counted her breaths. As her heart thumped more strongly, she could busy her brain with the complexities of counting paces, gasps, heartbeats, in their differing rates, all at once. Crowds and music thinned, stores became houses and flats. A few men huddled in doorways, their backs to her. Some of the shabby, long-windowed flats were already brightly lit, and through the open doorway of one came music and laughter. In the window of another, dingier flat was a sign FOR RENT $815 FIRST AND LAST MONTHS CLEANING DEPOSIT TWO BEDROOM. Her mind skipped over the outrageous figures, looking for the house number. Frank's address was 935, another three blocks.

The next block was even steeper. Here Castro Street was actually a valley between embankments, held back by tall concrete retaining walls. Beyond these gray walls, traversed by stairways, three-storey houses rose into the sky. Edging peaked roofs, or around windows, ornaments were painstakingly painted contrasting colors. Gardens were dug into the tall gray walls, sprouting well-trimmed bushes or spilling a cascade of purple blooming ice plant. A few young pepper trees lined the pavement, their branches arching just over Clara's head.

As she reached the crest of the hill, she realized she had forgotten the soup and fruit. But there was a small grocery and liquor store on the corner where she was able to get several cans. She picked out the best from what was left of over-ripe bananas and small early peaches and plums.

She recognized another late customer in the store. It was the woman in the green coat. She was quiet now. She cupped avocados gently in both hands, testing them for ripeness like any housewife. Now and then she murmured a few soft words to the bananas. She nodded at a brown, wilted cabbage. "Have to close up now, Myrtle." The woman dropped the avocados and scurried out, mumbling a bit louder, but looking neither at Clara nor the clerk. As Clara left with her purchases, he locked the door behind her and swung the sign around to show CLOSED through the glass window.

Beyond the store lay one short, level block before Castro Street plunged down steeply again. Through the darkening fog, Clara could see traffic and people three blocks below on Twenty-fourth Street, but here the street was deserted. She began to check the house numbers.

She had gone only a few steps when she stopped, numb, looking at the houses. It was like one of those dreams she still had occasionally, in which she played out a scene from her childhood or her marriage, the anguish sharpened by her present consciousness, her horror that perhaps she had not escaped after all. Escape had been only a dream. Reality was nightmare.

The houses covering half of the short block were six replicas of the house she had been born in, had married into. Narrow stucco boxes, squeezed together like a single, connected mass; identical stairways on the left leading to a window and door at the top; identical square garage doors with an identical trio of square windows above. Even the paint, washed out and dull in the fog, seemed the same gray-white under a faint tinge of color.

There was nothing uncanny about them. It was usual to see a row or group of identical houses in different parts of town, thrown up during the same year by the same builder, wherever a handy stretch of land was available.

The house numbered 935 differed from the others in only one way. Someone had crisscrossed the windows with dull gray strips of plastic to make them look like leaded glass. The plastic had already begun to peel off. She hesitated only a second at the foot of the steps, then quickly and quietly climbed them. Frank might be in the front bedroom, asleep just beyond the draped window next to the front door, which was exactly like the door of her parents' house, except that the handle had been painted gold and the doorbell removed, replaced by a massive door knocker. Clara clasped the door handle and gently pushed; the door swung open silently.

The living room drapes were drawn. The only light came through slits between them, a dim, foggy light from the street. But Clara knew that the door just to the left of the front door would lead to a bedroom. She stepped in, shutting the front door behind her. The bedroom door was open. She stepped toward the doorway and put her head through it.

"Hi, Mom."

He was sitting up in a large double bed, really a mattress and box spring laid on the floor against the wall where he leaned back against pillows. There was no other furniture. Boxes and suitcases filled most of the space. Empty bookshelves lay on their side against the thinly draped window. Books spilled out of several boxes, towels and sheets from another, as if Frank had been grabbing and using whatever he needed without ever actually unpacking.

From the doorway she could see his expression change from pleased greeting to a faint smile, which drooped as if his muscles were too weak to sustain it. His long face was Goyaesque, his thin, aquiline nose sharp and white above the dark stubble of his unshaved cheeks, sunken with sudden weight loss. His face looked unusually long and exposed because his hair was cut shorter than Clara had seen it for years, reduced almost to a black shadow around his forehead.

"Yellow, huh?"

Clara nodded.

"Good to see you."

Clara could not think of an answer. It was as if someone had greeted her in a foreign language, or one entirely inappropriate to the occasion, like praising her dress in the midst of a fire.

"A hell of a meeting after a whole year. But while you stand there admiring my good looks...you could say something." He wore a dingy robe under blankets pulled up to his chest. One arm lay outside the blankets, his hand lying palm up. His hands were broad, with thick, stubby fingers. It had always seemed to Clara that any sign of strength lay in Frank's hands, not in his tall but awkward frame. His exposed hand lay open, a bronze-tinged supplicant. It was that hand which expressed his illness, that and the heavy air in the room.

"It smells awful in here."

Frank sighed. "I sweat a lot." His eyes had always drooped slightly at the outer corners. Now the droop was exaggerated, though his eyes were opened wide, alert. "But my temperature stayed normal again all day, so I think I'm over the worst of it. And I'm hungry; that's a good sign. In between this funny pain in my gut, there are definite hunger pangs. It hurts mostly on this side, where..." He rolled over slightly as he described the sporadic pain, the nightmares that came whenever he dozed off, the changes in his skin, eyes, mucous membranes, bodily secretions. Clara half listened, half watched, gauging his apparent vigor, absorbing signs that although he might be weak, he was in no danger. "...and the fact that I'm starting to notice the stink must mean I'm better. I even feel like taking a shower, maybe shaving."

Clara heard her voice in automatic response. "You do that. While I'm fixing some food for you." Her voice seemed to come from a long way off, but evidently it sounded normal to Frank.

"Good idea. Then I'll look and feel more human, yellow or not."

She stayed in the doorway, watching him pull aside the covers and swing his long legs over the edge of the mattress. He had some trouble getting to his feet, and wavered unsteadily. Clara gripped the woodwork of the doorway, resisting the temptation to go to him and help him.

"Aren't you even going to come into the room?"

"Not until you're out of it."

"I'm probably not even contagious anymore."

"I'd rather not take a chance."

"Even if I were, you couldn't catch anything unless you kissed me."

Clara said nothing. Frank now stood steadily in the opposite doorway, which would lead down a short hallway to the bathroom. He looked very tall and narrow, his long arms and legs exposed outside the skimpy robe. Halfway through the doorway, he turned back. "Recognize the house? That guy must have built thousands of them." Not waiting for Clara's nod, he stepped into the hall, then disappeared, to his left, into the bathroom.

Clara moved swiftly, high-stepping and dodging between boxes, pulling the drapes open, unlocking the window and heaving it upward. Then she stripped the bed, handling the sheets as little as possible, with fingertips, before flinging them into a corner. Quickly she put fresh sheets on the bed.

She followed through the doorway Frank had used, but turned right instead of left, toward the kitchen. She raised her hand to where she knew the light switch would be. It illuminated a stained glass ball which cast a motley green light over a butcher's block table. Above the table and against the small window over the sink hung thick ferns, their drooping fronds catching the green light. Tendrils of ivy hung down from pots hooked to the ceiling. A small, messy table held leftover food, used cups, magazines, a miniature television. A single chair stood beside it, turned away as if its occupant

120

had just risen and left. Evidently the owner of this house—
like Clara's parents—spent most of his time in the kitchen.

Clara went to the sink and washed her hands. Then she
turned on the broiler, took the fish from the refrigerator, cut
off a large piece, and put it on a flat pan. Rummaging in
cabinets she found another pan, then opened a can of soup
and started it slowly heating up on the stove. She saw only
one tray, standing up against the wall behind the sink. It was
black with red and gold figures on it, like something copied
from an ancient Grecian urn. Naked male figures in helmets,
boots, and bracelets thrust erect penises or bent forward to
receive them. Clara covered the figures with paper towels, on
which she placed fruit, bread, and dishes for the soup and
fish. She washed her hands again, soaping them well and
using a paper towel to dry them.

The sound of cascading water stopped. Frank would be
out of the shower, drying. Short spurts of water meant he was
shaving, brushing his teeth. She put the fish under the broiler,
leaned back against the wall, brushing away the tendrils of
ivy which touched her cheek. The green light made her hands
livid; she shuddered and pushed open the door to the dining
room.

A massive table, china cabinet, buffet and six chairs almost filled the small room, like a huddle of dark, heavy,
crouching animals. A move in any direction, Clara felt, would
make her stumble over them. She reached back to the wall
and touched the light switch. A dim amber glow came from
cone-shaped bulbs in a massive wrought-iron chandelier
hanging above the table. What light the huge fixture gave
did little more than spread shadows of itself, black coils spread-
ing across the ceiling and down the walls.

It did cast some light on a tapestry hanging on the wall
above the buffet. Clara moved around the table, squeezing
between chairs and buffet to look at it. The tapestry depicted

a group of men, clearly a Biblical scene. One of the men was grasping and kissing another, whose head was surrounded by a halo. Behind them stood unheeded, menacing soldiers with weapons raised. It must be Jesus in the garden, with Judas delivering the kiss of betrayal, marking Jesus for the soldiers' attack. Yet something about the scene was not right. It was the expression of the two embracing men. There was no duplicity in the face of Judas, only the purest love, and the soldiers seemed to be menacing both men. The tapestry looked very old, but when Clara leaned over the buffet and fingered it, she touched a synthetic fabric—a new tapestry, faded and stained, artificially aged.

The dining room light switch had activated a dim glow from the living room. She walked across the bare wood floors, four steps taking her into the small living room. There was a red plush sofa and, beside it, one straight-backed, black wooden chair with a red plush cushion seat. Between the two seats stood a low, pink marble-topped table. Clara sat down on the chair.

On the table lay three books and a small marble statue, a rounded, smooth figure like a Bufano seal. At second glance, Clara saw it was a human figure in a monk's cassock, lying prone, its praying hands and wide-eyed face raised with a fervency that seemed slightly comic. Clara picked up one of the books. It was bound in white leather. The thin pages were gilt-edged and covered with markings like no language Clara had ever seen. They looked parched and aged, but in some way fake. And there was something strange about the chair Clara sat in. It was too high for her feet to touch the floor, and so narrow that its edge cut across her thighs. When Clara leaned back, she was prodded at kidney level by ornamental knobs set at precisely the point to create discomfort. She glanced toward the little fireplace. Like her parents' fireplace, it was unused. It had been painted pale gold inside, almost the color of Frank's jaundiced hand.

The dim light came from above the fireplace, from the mantel where a candle-shaped lamp lit up what was clearly the centerpiece of the room: a huge crucifix. The wooden cross, painted deep gray, stood on the mantel and reached to the ceiling. The grotesquely contorted figure hanging from it was painted in garish colors, with blood-red rivulets running from wounds in the hands, feet, and side. From the forehead, beneath spiky black thorns, red drops spread and ran in thin lines down the twisted face, with its eyes and mouth opened in agony, its black beard and hair bristling. Clara recognized the authenticity of the crucifix. She had seen others like it in remote village churches in Mexico, where it expressed the primitive fervency and the deep suffering of the people who worshiped there. Here it looked ferocious.

She felt a rocking sensation, like a slight, silent earthquake, then a darkening. Closing her eyes, she quickly leaned forward, elbows on her knees, head drooping. She had fainted only once in her life, when she got up too quickly right after Frank's birth. She remembered the first sign, the darkening. A sick feeling grew from the center of her body, a hot, boiling void, an emptiness that raged. It made a roaring in her ears, a hollow sound that mixed with the sound of water splashes coming from the bathroom. "It's because I didn't eat my lunch," she mumbled between her knees. She kept her head down until there were no more sounds from the bathroom.

Then she got up, went back to the kitchen, and turned the fish. She poured the soup into a bowl, added a glass of water to the tray, and as she heard the bathroom door open, took the fish out of the oven and put it on the dish. She took the tray into Frank's room and put it on the box of books beside the bed. She closed the window on the well-aired room and left it.

She went through the living room and dining room to the kitchen, turning out the lights as she passed, and washing her hands once more. She looked for a glass, then remembered

Arthur's warning and cupped her hand under the faucet, bending her face to it and sucking up the water. She cupped her hand again and again, sucking greedy mouthfuls, smearing her wet hand across her forehead and around her neck.

When she came back, taking up her place in the doorway, Frank was in bed, already eating. He had put on a striped T-shirt under his robe. He had shaved, but had left a dark shadow on his upper lip, an incipient moustache. She leaned against the door frame.

"Great! Clean sheets, good food. I always said there's nothing like an Italian mama." At her silence, he looked up from his food. "Hey, that's a joke, remember? Our joke." At Clara's nod, Frank sighed and began to eat again. "Well, you could talk to me while I eat. You won't catch anything just by opening your mouth."

Remember what you said to me about Hartzler? How you felt a huge space opening between you, too wide for communication?

Right. I guess it's hard to imagine.

I'm beginning to.

What? You don't have to whisper. You look tired. You really should sit somewhere.

How did you end up in this place?

A notice on a bulletin board. But I have to get out.

Because you're contagious?

No, he's had it. He's immune.

Of course.

He won't let me put my things anywhere but in this room. As for sitting on one of his precious antique chairs

Arthur says he could find you something in the Richmond.

Way out there? I might as well live in Canada.

I can't imagine you'd want to use any room but this. The rest of the house is like a mausoleum.

Yeah, pretty awful, isn't it? But a lot of antique art is religious.

And a lot of it isn't. And a lot of this stuff is fake. What is this thing gay people have with Jesus?

I suppose they see certain parallels. Some people see the history of gay people as one long crucifixion.

And wallow in it? Furnish their homes with it?

Well, don't pin my landlord's taste on all gays.

Then there are those men who dress as nuns, and that quartet that sings parodies of hymns.

Social protest. You ought to be able to understand that. We learned protest songs based on black spirituals, remember, when we used to picket the five-and-dime in Berkeley because blacks couldn't get a cup of coffee in their branch in Mississippi.

I don't understand what this protest is aimed at.

You ought to. You used to tell me how the nuns waited for you after school, chased you down Mission Street like big, black vampire bats, threatening you with hell because you wouldn't go to church.

That was forty years ago. Nuns don't dress that way anymore. Or act that way. At least I don't think they do. The only nuns I hear of now are the ones killed by some right-wing death squad in Latin America.

So the habits are a bit dated. But the spirit of satire

The spirit of this satire seems dated too. That quartet sang about Jesus as cock-sucker. When I was thirteen, the kids used to sing songs like that, worse ones about the nuns. A few years later they got married in church and sent their kids to schools run by the nuns.

Which you refused to do. Okay. That's you and me. But you have to realize that most of the gay community has come here from somewhere else, from places where people like Reverend Gynt run things. Where gays have been told all their lives that they are filthy and evil and God will punish them. The new attack on gay people is mobilized through

125

those conservative churches, those old middle-American Bible thumpers. Gay people are rejected by family and community and friends, all in the name of God. And what's this quartet?

I went to the benefit show at the Castro. They opened the program.

Good turnout?

Packed.

Damn, and I missed it. Was it good? How was the movie?

I don't know. I left in the middle of Arnold Scott's act. You know who he is?

Oh, sure, he's gathering quite a following. Benjy and Colin took me to see him the night after I got back. To celebrate.

I hadn't seen him for twenty-five years. I thought he was dead.

Oh, you used to go see him?

Once.

You never told me. Was his act the same then?

Less hostile toward women.

Oh, come on, he'll bait anyone if he's in the mood. Could I have some more bread?

There isn't any more. When I saw Arnold Scott twenty-five years ago, he did an imitation of female glamour, invented by men, for heterosexual men, tourists from Reverend Gynt's territory. Now he tells jokes about "stupid cunts."

You're just picking on one little thing.

It was the one little thing that went over biggest. With an audience of young gay men, not those old straight salesmen from the uptight fifties. It was the climax of his act.

For you. Because you left. If you hadn't been so touchy, if you'd waited for

I left with every other woman in that theater. Including the entire Lesbian Chorus—members of the gay community this show was supposed to benefit. The show went right on,

126

after the cheering that accompanied our exit. As if our exit was the best part.

Hey, you're really angry, aren't you? I don't see why you'd get so excited about Arnold Scott.

Not about him, Frank; it's his audience. The old stereotype about gay men was that they deeply hated women. Then gay liberation said that wasn't true. Gay men didn't hate anyone. They just wanted freedom from persecution. So—there I was in a theater where gay people were free to express themselves as they truly are. And what came out was hostility toward women that actually frightened me.

Well, sure, there are some strains between gay men and lesbians. But it's all part of that other thing too, the over-reaction of these young guys from middle America. It's not really anti-woman; it's just a lot of negative emotion that gets released when you've been hounded by the law, beaten up by other kids, rejected by your family, scared of

Yes, Frank, but what does that have to do with you? I never sent you to the nuns or to any church. I never forced women on you. No one beat you up in school—you were bigger than all of them. I didn't disown you when you told me you

I don't follow you. What's your question?

I looked around that theater and I wondered which of those men were your friends—these names I hear without ever having faces attached to them. Benjy and Colin are the latest in dozens of names that come and go.

Benjy's blonde, your height, but slight, about twenty, with

Don't bother. I wouldn't have been able to pick him out. Those men all looked alike. When the women got up and left, only a few men followed. If you hadn't been sick, if you had been there with your friends, and you had seen the women get up and leave, would you have gotten up too and left? Or would you have been cheering and stomping and screaming and laughing and

I don't know what's wrong with you. I've never seen you like this. Look, whatever is the matter with you, I'm sick. I don't want to argue some hypothetical crap about what I would have done someplace where I wasn't. Are you having problems at the college again? If you're upset about them, don't take it out on me.

I'm upset about you.

I know. I appreciate your feelings. You're frightened for me. I wasn't exactly happy with the news. You're concerned for me. But you see I'm going to be all right. Don't make a big thing out of it.

It is a big thing. People die of hepatitis. Or they suffer long-term liver damage. Or they go into chronic, incurable illness. Why didn't that quartet sing a funny song about a hepatitis carrier selling his blood to make serum to protect his lovers against him? Wouldn't that have been funnier than monogamous lesbians?

Thanks. Thanks a lot. That's just what I need to think about while I'm trying to recover.

Or a song about some of the diseases in this pamphlet. How about the "Gay Bowel Boogie"? or "Herpes Forever"?

Oh, that thing. So that's what's freaking you out. Look, if it will set your mind at ease, I haven't used anything stronger than pot since college, and I'm not about to rim any stranger. You know I never cruised toilets, and leather bars and that stuff are just stupid.

But your friends do.

That's their business.

And you think you can be with people who do these things and not be affected?

I'm careful.

I see. Do you make love with the lights on, checking for rashes and sores? How romantic.

You don't know anything about it.

I know you've caught a serious disease.

Anyone can catch hepatitis. You could catch it from a dirty glass, from food cooked by an Asian immigrant at Arthur's favorite restaurant on Clement Street, what's its name? Or from

But that's not how you caught it, Frank. You caught it from a sex contact at the baths, didn't you? Because you said to me, "Well, you wouldn't want me to become a monk." That means you know you caught it through sex.

So I was unlucky.

Just living here is pushing your luck. Frank, do you know the significance of that question you asked? "You don't want me to become a monk?" That question implies just two alternatives, celibacy or disease. You're telling me you choose disease. You equate gay sex life with disease.

I'm not telling you anything. You're doing all the talking.

If I had only those two choices, I would choose celibacy. But, in fact, there are not only those two choices. Wait. Bear with me. Listen. Do you remember the night you told me you were gay? At fifteen? Half your life ago?

Yes, and you freaked out then too.

What did I say?

Not much. That you loved me. While you were turning green. It was written all over you. You might have gay friends, but you didn't want a gay son.

True. But for a parent of those days I didn't do too badly. Do you remember what we did that night?

I'm too tired for all this.

You went to your room and brought out stacks of gay pornography. I had no idea—the modern parent who would never dream of going through your mail or your room. You showed it to me, and we talked about how this stuff exploited you and your desires.

While you turned even greener at seeing explicit gay sexuality. And then you burned it.

We burned it. Sitting on the floor in front of the fireplace.

As if you could dispose of my feelings so easily. I half believed it myself. But they all came back, just as the porno came back, I was on so many lists. And then you begged me not to make a pass at anyone, not yet, not yet.

Yes. There was the law. And you can't have forgotten what your high school was like in 1965, no matter how big you were. So when you went away to college I started to get ready for the next step. To conquer my prejudice. To get ready to welcome, with open arms, your lover, when you brought him home.

Well. Go on.

But you never did. Never. In the dozen years since you left home, there has never been a lover, one person, for even a year, for even a few months. I thought it was just a stage—the bars and the baths—but the years went by and the stage never ended. That pornography we threw into the fire, that was your definition of being gay.

What if it is?

Frank, that's the same definition Hartzler gives, or Reverend Gynt, or all those Bible-thumping reactionaries, all those enemies of yours and mine. Speaking of Bible thumpers, maybe the Bible *has something. Maybe in cities where promiscuous sodomy was common, intestinal diseases spread like a curse and wiped them out. Do you suppose that's the real meaning of God destroying the city of Sodom? Wrapped up in all that mean, joyless hatred of sex the Bible thumpers give us, is there one tiny grain of truth—that promiscuity equals disease?*

Next you'll be saying "the wages of sin is death." You must be going crazy if you quote the *Bible* on health.

This pamphlet isn't the Bible *or a religious tract. It's a medical pamphlet, written by gay doctors.*

Which is already dated. Pretty soon that serum will be available, and hepatitis will be wiped out, like smallpox. Same with the others.

There are new strains of syphilis and gonorrhea, resistant to antibiotics. And Arthur told me about

Look, there are always risks in every life that's worth living. You always say how Grandma and Grandpa lived in constant fear, never took risks, and ended up sitting in their kitchen, polishing the woodwork and counting their money, and how you didn't want to live that way.

How can you take what I say and twist it into a justification for wasting your life?

Mom, I've had enough of this. I don't want any more talk of disease or any other scare tactic to push me into celibacy or monogamy or some other conventional straight jacket.

You used to tell me you wanted a single relationship if you could only find the right one.

That's right. I had the same brainwashing as you. For me it would be boy meets boy and lives happily ever after. But that's just a new version of the same old oppressive family pattern. You fought out of it, and I've just carried the fight further. I'm not ever going to be a husband and a father, so why should I drag along all the baggage that goes with the family? Some of those old queers settled down with a mate and a house mortgage and a boring job, and all those things they didn't know they could be free of. Polishing the woodwork and counting their money just like your parents. Why in hell be gay if you're just going to be straight everywhere but in bed? Why not be free?

I agree

Well, you sure as hell don't sound like it.

But free to do what?

I'm working on the answer to that question. That's why I came back here.

To be free to screw more? A series of anonymous sexual encounters, one after another, with no stable relationship? Is that freedom? It sounds more boring than monogamy. And more lonely.

I'm not alone. I have friends. That's the difference you can't understand. In your day, you met lots of people, but had no sex with them. Because sex was such a profound, problematical thing, procreation and so on. You had to pick one person and give up all the other possible varieties of experience. You had to put everything into that relation with that one sex partner and

I never put everything into

Wait a minute. You've been doing all the talking. Now let me have my say. You put everything into the relation with that one sex partner, all energy, support, love, time, all of it caged and tamed till passion dried up. We keep our passion uncaged. Cruising, promiscuity, call it whatever you want. By having multiple sex contacts—yes, hundreds, why not?—we refuse the deadening of passion. We live in a constant high. You think that's easy? You think it doesn't call for a dedication like a religious vocation? Oh, I can't make you understand. The only people who can understand are those who live it, who have the courage to pitch their lives at

But sex isn't the only way to

Through sex we're maintaining that razor edge of heightened life, total awareness, the excitement that life was meant to be. And we'll go through sex to a joyous freedom society hasn't ever known. We're the vanguard, and through what you call our promiscuity, we are becoming a brotherhood, bonded in

Larry died alone.

Larry who?

I don't believe a word of that, and I don't think you believe it either. And while you're rattling it off like some party line, some catechism you memorized, only one answer comes into my head: "The expense of spirit in a waste of shame is

132

Really! Are you going to claim Shakespeare as well as the Bible on your side? You must need help pretty badly. Probably because the promiscuity that so offends your residual puritanism is just what everyone wants. You read my interview with Hartzler. It reeked with envy of freedom from monogamy and family. Fucking whenever and whomever you want is every man's fantasy.

Are you saying you want to live out everyman's fantasy?

Touché, Mom, touché. I'm not quite up to a really sharp battle of wits today.

Frank, this isn't a contest, it's...shall I tell you what I hoped you'd do with your freedom from monogamy and family?

Yes, you shall, whether or not I want to hear it.

My mother used to say, "Raising a child is the hardest work in the world. If you could put all that energy into some other work, you'd rise to the top in whatever it was." It was all in that repeated statement, her hatred of her marriage, of motherhood, of all the duties she tried to pass on to me. I felt her resentment so deeply. That's why I wouldn't wait until you were grown before I started teaching. I didn't want to resent you that way. And when I got used to your being gay, I used to think, Frank will be able to put all the energy he has into his work. Like the artists Hartzler mentioned. Not that nonsense about unsatisfied sexual energy left over. Simply that you had more time and energy to concentrate on yourself, your talent. You were free to be the best. But that isn't how you've used that freedom. You've used it to hop from one thing to another. You have been as promiscuous in your use of your talent as you have been in your sex life, and as trivial. You waste your freedom. Your whole life is cruising.

That's a lie. Every kind of work I've tried has been a great passion, a love affair stronger than anything in my sex life.

But none ever turned into commitment.

No, they burned out, and then I quit rather than go on with the taste of ashes in my mouth. So I never made a name for myself with some brilliant career that would justify your life.

That's not fair. I'm not that kind of mother. But even if I were—is that so bad? Is it so bad for a mother to want her son to become the best of whatever fine things are in him?

Your raving has carried you past the point of decency. You can't talk to me as if I were a twelve-year-old. You seem to forget that I'm thirty years old.

No, I don't forget. I've thought of nothing else all day, that you're thirty, not eighteen. I even ask myself that old trite question, how did I feel at thirty? There's no way to compare. At thirty I was the mother of a ten-year-old boy and had been teaching for six years.

And at thirty you left Dad, split the family, went and made your own life. And your parents ranted at you the same way, telling you that you were throwing away your life.

It's not the same.

But it is. Every generation does it. The mother has to learn to let go.

My mother was trying to hold me to a pattern, a prison that I had to break out of.

So are you.

I am not. I was fighting to open up my life. You want to close yours.

You judge me out of your ignorance, just as she did. That's why I can't be really angry at you. Maybe you can't help it. The psychological process is classic. What's amazing to me is that you should fall into it.

Can't a mother ever be right? If I saw you getting ready to jump out of a window and screamed, would that just be another example of the generation gap?

You know, I'm amazed. I can't believe this. If anyone had ever told me you'd act just like...like a mother, I'd have laughed at them. I don't understand how

And you never will. You'll never have children so you'll never know what I'm going through. I'm as amazed as you. I couldn't have imagined it before today. I was so well-trained, self-taught to be the well-behaved, liberal parent, eyes and mouth shut, until

Jesus, if this is going to be a speech about breaking a mother's heart, spare me. It's not only incredible, it's such poor theater, all this melodrama just because I've come home.

It's your reason for coming home—that you won't live anywhere you have to "deny your sexuality." Does that mean you can live only on one little dot on the globe? Is that what gay freedom is? The need to live in this ghetto?

The need to live in a community of my own kind.

Frank, I fought to get out of this place, to get free of a community of people who tried to make me their kind. I was fighting for my life.

Good, fine, so you got away and found your life and your own kind up there in the redwoods.

When did I ever say that? I've worked with groups for a common goal. I've made some friends. But...my own kind? There's no such thing. Unless you narrow yourself down to... if you call gay people your own kind, you're narrowing yourself down to define yourself by your sexuality. You're doing what all those oppressors of gay people have done. You define yourself as they do.

Now I see what's wrong with you. You've never really accepted my being gay. Deep down you're just like any homophobe. You're afraid your son is going to turn into some flaming queen like Arnold Scott.

Arnold Scott? But he's a very good flaming queen. He's worked very hard to make the most of what he is. I'm afraid

*you won't be like him. I'm afraid you're going to make nothing
out of what you are.*

Look, I'm in the middle of a very difficult, very traumatic
transition. I need moral support, not all this hysterical trash.
I came back thinking I had a place to stay and it fell through.
Theo promised me a consulting job, and it fell through. This
room is costing a fortune. I'm running out of money, and I
won't be able to work for weeks. And when I do, I'll be lucky
if Benjy can get me on with him at the restaurant where he
works.

Dear God, another gay waiter.

This is incredible. I'm sick and weak, and you pick this
time to argue with me.

*Because it may be my only chance. I tried to hold back,
but I realized I've been holding back for years, since your
first dose of syphilis. Now, while you're weak and in pain and
afraid—there must be something left of the fear you felt
when you called me—maybe you'll hear what I'm saying.*

You just saw a few of the problems here and you panicked.
You can't see the promise of the future. This is just a phase.
In the long run

We live in the short run.

a new way of life will come out of gay sexuality.

*Sexuality has nothing to do with it. All that talk is a cover
for something else. For fear, for lack of nerve and stamina.
Life demands both. It demands commitment and endurance
and work that sometimes is hard and boring. If you're going
to build a life. That's what growing up is.*

Now you sound like Hartzler. Well, fuck growing up, as
you call it.

*Exactly. Fuck it. Fuck it and start all over again, forever a
boy. Peter Pan with gonorrhea up his ass. You've come back
to live in a place where stores have names like All American*

Boy, with display windows full of teddy bears, where fifty-year-old men walk around in split-fly jeans, all boyish muscles from the neck down, wrinkles above, and rot inside. If this is a community, it's as uniform and oppressive as the one I got out of when I left here. These men even look the way men did in the fifties. Freedom? God, that crazy woman on the street is right. It is a rebellion against God, against yourself. It's suicide.

I think I'm beginning to understand you.

Are you? Oh, Frank, I only want

Yes. I understand now. Remember this morning, when you were down in the BART tube, afraid to come up? Afraid you couldn't handle seeing the Mission again, after all you went through here when you were young. You've never really resolved any of that. That's why you stayed away all these years. Coming here today was a mistake. No, it was probably good, in the long run, because it exposed all the pain you're still carrying inside. That's better than going on repressing it. I wish I could help, but what you really need is to get into therapy. No, please, don't say anymore. I'm bushed, I need rest. I appreciate your coming, and thanks for the food. After I get well and settled in a new place, and find a job, I'll call you. Maybe then I'll take a drive up and see you. Please go now. Think about what I said. And take care of yourself.

Except for short and frustrating forays in search of more money or a car that would start, the four young men had hardly left the red brick bench of the BART station. The beer had given out an hour ago. Ramon had vomited once, and the others had shunned him for his stinking waste of good beer. But Chico did not send him away, because Ramon had paid for most of the beer, and because it was more fun to defend him and laugh at the revulsion and disapproval of passersby. Julio and Al began once or twice to move threateningly toward those disapproving looks, but Chico only let them shout a few obscene challenges, calling them back when they started to follow anyone.

Their plans, a short list of limited possibilities named without enthusiasm and never pursued, had narrowed down to the idea of waiting until dark, then moving west of Mission Street toward queer territory. The big parade had spilled thousands of fags onto Castro Street. By dark the ones left on the street would be stoned out of their senses. The stuff Julio had brought did nothing when added to their beer. He had probably been cheated again, ending up with nothing but pulverized aspirin mixed with sugar. But the faggots would be carrying good stuff, along with money. Chico gave a low whistle that brought back Julio and Al; then he indicated by a short nod, sideways toward the library, that it was dark enough to start up Twenty-fourth Street.

Ramon, anxious to regain some manhood after the ignominy of being sick, began to mutter about cutting up a queer, then smashing his pretty face. "Shut up, man." Ramon was instantly quiet, watching Chico without resentment.

Chico's authority was unquestioned because it was said that on the last Gay Pride Day, he had killed a man. It was in all the papers that a queer on Castro Street had suddenly slumped and died in the dark, a knife wound through his heart, no one in the thick crowds having any idea who had killed him. The rumor was that Chico was the killer. No one knew for sure, except Al, who had been with Chico that night, and he would not talk about it. Slowly the conviction grew and spread: Chico had done it. In recent months Chico's quiet air of authority had deepened, like a wordless statement that he had indeed killed. They all deferred to him now, took their orders from him.

Chico knew they could no longer do anything so simple as walking up to mingle with the crowds. Ever since the killing, the fairies were more watchful, careful. It was too easy to spot Chico and his boys among them. Even the police acted less pleased about faggot cutting—they were even, it was said, recruiting faggot cops. Pressure was on from City Hall. The cops knew Chico, had questioned him about the killing. So it was too risky to go right up onto Castro Street. It was no good even up at Dolores Park, near the high school. Too many people up there knew them. Besides, the fags kept out of the park after dark now, since so many had got their heads kicked.

Chico explained the plan: they would move a little way up Twenty-fourth Street, then off onto the side streets near Church or Sanchez. They would keep their eyes open for an empty street, a lone queer—at most a couple—leaving Castro. They would hit him fast for money and dope, and leave him quiet. Chico was stern-eyed when he said, "quiet," and the others were ashamed to betray any qualms by asking if he meant they were to leave him unconscious or dead. They all carried knives, which they had often drawn, but never used—but that was a secret each held more closely than he would if he had killed.

Now they moved silently up Twenty-fourth Street, past the darkened library, avoiding the lighted, crowded coffee house across the street. On the next block there was no one except three lesbians loading some stuff into a car. Chico shook his head. One alone they might rape, to teach her a lesson. But in a group lesbians were wary and tough, likely to start screeching, blowing whistles, and throwing things before you even got near. Besides, they never had any money. The three women had seen them and were already hustling into the car and driving away.

The next block was completely deserted, a closed-up limbo of apartments with blank doors at street level, the high walls of the Catholic school, not even an open stairway where people might linger. Once they crossed Dolores Street there would be more shops and restaurants, and people. Probably now was as good a time as any to turn up a side street.

They were just turning off when Chico saw her. He stopped, glanced back, but motioned the others to stay where they were, up Quane Alley, close to the building. Then he edged back around the corner to look.

He remembered her at once. She was the woman they had seen at the BART station earlier in the day. She wore jeans and short hair like the lesbians taking over Valencia Street, but she wasn't one of them. She was old, about fifty, and she didn't live around here. She had come on BART and was walking back to BART. Probably she lived across the bay, one of those dykes who came over from Berkeley. She had watched Chico closely at the BART station. Her gaze had been level, even, unafraid, and sad. She made him feel small. It seemed only right that now she should reappear, in the dark, on an empty street, fated for his revenge. Besides, she would have money. The old out-of-town dykes always did.

He gathered the other three close to the building, instructing them with few words, glaring at Ramon's face with contempt, until he wiped off the expression which showed some scruples about raping a woman older than his mother. Only her money, he gestured, an easy take. In more quick gestures he silently told them that he would only have to show her the knife, and the others could stay back unless he needed them. When he had her money, he would signal, and they must run, run, because within a block or two there were people whose attention she could arouse if she yelled.

Chico stayed back behind the building with them. He planned to wait until she had walked past, then come up behind her. He took out his knife and touched the point to his lips, like a finger raised to hush the other three, to impose utter silence while they listened for her footsteps.

He could not hear them. She was one of those women who did not dress like a woman, who wore quiet, flat shoes, with rubbery contact with the concrete, soundless. He would have

142

to be careful. Such women, even an old one like this, were sometimes stronger than they looked. He knew he could count on the others to help if she gave trouble.

But suddenly he saw that if they had to come to his aid—against an old woman—he would lose his authority over them. It would be better to shove the knife into her than to let even one of them come to help him. What if she turned and saw him? recognized him? The police were looking for an excuse to pick him up again, and she, having watched him so intently before, would provide a positive identification of a mug shot. He felt pressures closing in around him. It was like the last time, all these unforeseen circumstances coming together at once, forcing him to a decision, creating the act and using him as the tool to commit it.

Now he heard sounds, but not footsteps, something like low talking or a strange singing. He froze against the side of the building. Wasn't she alone? He was sure she had been when he first saw her. No one could have joined her in this deserted block. He hated to poke his head around the corner to see, lest she—or whoever she was talking to—should see him. He poised himself for the quickest possible motion of his head, the briefest glance.

Quickly he darted a portion of his head, one eye, past the corner of the building and drew it as quickly back. He blinked. Then he moved his head outward again, slowly, in the most leisurely way, not bothering to pull back, not bothering to hide at all.

She was alone. Her wide eyes and wet cheeks caught glimmers from the lone street light. Her eyes stared straight ahead, obviously seeing nothing. Her breathing had become grating sobs, blurring the sounds her mouth made, sounds which Chico had mistaken for conversation with a companion. Her legs moved steadily as if they had been wound up and set to plod mechanically forward, carrying her heavy, stiff body.

Chico stepped forward in full view of her, and she did not see him. She muttered and sobbed as she plodded blindly on.

"Christ, another *loca*," he muttered, leaning back against the building. The other three moved up close to huddle behind him and watch her go by. Stupid Julio even crossed himself, too shaken to notice Chico's sigh of relief. Chico smiled and shrugged. No one expected him to go near her. They all felt a superstitious chill at the sight of these people, like Myrtle, the old one in the green coat who was always out there yelling at the faggots. Sometimes they cheered Myrtle on, but they would no more have touched her than they would touch a leper. This one was even saying the same crazy stuff, about "my son, my son." It must be catching.

Chico laughed as he closed his knife and put it away. Then he signaled the others with a nod of his head as he turned again up the side street. They followed him obediently.

BOOKS BY DOROTHY BRYANT

Novels

ELLA PRICE'S JOURNAL (paper) $6

THE KIN OF ATA ARE WAITING FOR YOU (paper) $5

MISS GIARDINO (paper) $6

THE GARDEN OF EROS (paper) $6

PRISONERS (paper) $6
 (cloth) $10

KILLING WONDER (paper) $6
 (cloth) $10

A DAY IN SAN FRANCISCO (paper $6
 (cloth) $12

Non-fiction

WRITING A NOVEL (paper) $5

PLEASE WRITE FOR CURRENT PRICES

$1 covers postage for any size order
Californians please add 6% sales tax
Order from

ATA BOOKS
1928 Stuart Street, Berkeley, California 94703